Praise for Annmarie McKenna's *Checkmate*

5 Nymphs "Checkmate is a wonderful paranormal romance. ...Ms. McKenna spins a superb tale full of intriguing characters. The healthy dose of action and suspense added to the mix will have readers at the edge of their seats as a murderer closes in for his next victim."

~ Water Nymph, Literary Nymphs

5 Shamrocks "If you have already read Annmarie McKenna's first shape shifter story, *Seeing Eye Mate*, then you must be panting like wolf for the sequel to that story, *Checkmate*! McKenna did a fine job of teasing us thoroughly with just enough about Caelan's identical twin brother, Eli, to leave us salivating for more! And she does not let the readers down with *Checkmate*. Both Eli and the plot far surpassed my greatest expectations, and left me hungry for yet another sequel!"

~ Jennifer, CK2S Kwips and Kritiques

Blue Ribbon Rating 4 "I can't begin to express how much I loved this story. I was so engrossed in the book that any noise I heard had me jumping in fear! Ms McKenna did an excellent job of developing her characters and keeping me in suspense. I felt as if I were right there in the same room watching the action as the story unfolded. In addition to this wonderful plot, the identity of the killer came as a complete shock. Annmarie McKenna has written another riveting novel and I am simply delighted with her storytelling abilities."

~ *Shayla, Romance Junkies*

5 Stars "What a beautiful story! Checkmate had some of everything that I like in astory—werewolves, hot steamy sex, and suspense. Ms. McKenna even had meguessing 'who did it' until the very end...BRAVO!... There were so manytwist and turns in the story, but they worked and I was able to keep up andI loved it. I am looking forward to reading more great work from Ms. McKenna."

~ *LT Blue, Just Erotic Romance Reviews*

Checkmate

Annmarie McKenna

A Samhain Publishing, Ltd. publication.

Samhain Publishing, Ltd.
512 Forest Lake Drive
Warner Robins, GA 31093
www.samhainpublishing.com

Checkmate
Copyright © 2007 by Annmarie McKenna
Print ISBN: 1-59998-626-4
Digital ISBN: 1-59998-326-5

Editing by Sasha Knight
Cover by Scott Carpenter

First Samhain Publishing, Ltd. electronic publication: February 2007
First Samhain Publishing, Ltd. print publication: August 2007

Dedication

I've got to send this one out to my sister, my editor, whom I love and should probably add her name to the front cover, and to everyone who asked for Eli's story and felt I'd done him wrong in *Seeing Eye Mate*. Thanks!

Chapter One

"Well what have we got here?"

Nicole Raine Taylor hesitated a split second and whipped her gaze toward the leering voice coming from her right. Her heart thumped once, twice, before settling into a more normal rhythm. The group of three young men hanging out by the open sliding door of a ratty van couldn't be talking to her.

Keep walking. Don't stop. No sense in giving them a reason to talk to her.

From the corner of her eye she saw the one who'd been leaning against the car next to the van stand straighter. She twisted her keys in her hand until they poked out between the clenched fingers of her fist.

Picking up the pace, Nikki hurried to the cherry red Jeep Wrangler she'd bought six months earlier. It was parked not more than fifteen or sixteen spots away. No problem.

"Where you goin', pretty girl?"

Problem. Heavy footsteps sounded behind her along with a whistled catcall. Damn it. If only she'd thought to grab her cell phone out of her bag before leaving the Maxwell's Department Store end of Scenic Rivers Mall.

Stupid. Too damn stupid to live.

Shit. Not a good thought to have under the circumstances. She swallowed back the fear threatening to choke her and walked faster. With her free hand, Nikki reached into the bag swung over her shoulder and across her chest. Thunder vibrated the air, rumbling off in the distance. Prophetic.

"Lookin' for yer phone, little girl?" asked another raspy-voiced male. Someone else cackled.

"That is one mighty sweet ass."

"Hell yeah. I wish I had me some ass like that."

Fuck. How many more spots? Twelve? Fifteen? Short of breaking into a run and urging on their little game, what could she do?

Scream bloody murder.

She jerked her gaze around the parking lot. No one. How could there be no one in this parking lot right now? And why the hell had she talked Derek out of those karate lessons? Obviously her brother knew better than her.

It wasn't even completely dark yet. What did they think they were going to get away with?

"I asked you a question."

Nikki startled at the low growl directly behind her and broke into a sprint, her shrill scream echoing across the lot. Not two feet from her destination, one of the men lunged at her, slamming her into the Jeep and crushing her into the crevice between the spare tire and the rear door. Her keys stabbed into her ribs just below her left breast. A huge hand smashed her face into the glass that made up part of the black removable hardtop. Pain radiated through her cheek.

Filthy, garlicky, garbage breath washed over her mouth and nose from between the massive fingers covering the half of her face not squished against glass.

"You thought you was gonna get away, didn't you, sweet thing?"

His tongue traced her ear and bile rose in her esophagus.

She whimpered in disgust. The hand with her only weapon, her keys, was still trapped. The sharp metal gouged into the delicate skin between her fingers. Tears sprung beneath her eyelids.

"You give us what we want, we won't hurt you. You hear me, little girl?"

Shit. Shit, shit, shit. She readied herself to scream again. Her chest welled with the intake of breath needed.

His fingers grasped her mouth in a crushing pinch, yanking her head farther to the side than its normal turning capacity.

"I said, did you hear me?" he hissed and shook her face.

As if he didn't already have her attention. Nikki attempted to nod. The man released her chin and patted her cheek.

"Good girl."

Christ what could she do? A sharp twinge zinged across her ribs, bringing her focus back to the keys in her hand.

Not your only weapon. You have feet, knees, a brain. *Use them!*

The rasp of a zipper sounded behind her. The dirty, foul-smelling hand returned to cover her face. His fingertips pressed into her eyelids while his palm prevented her from yelling out again.

"Wouldn't want you to see us, now would we?"

You dumb sonofabitch, I already have.

Where the hell was everybody?

"Push her between the cars, Marco." The excited voice practically danced in her ears.

Marco, Marco, Marco. Nikki committed the name to memory. If she came out of this alive at least she had a name to go with the faces they foolishly thought she hadn't seen.

No. No! Nikki scrambled through her brain. This would not happen. Jesus, how would she ever face Eli again? She needed him. For once in her life she needed him more than wanted him, and he'd gone away on an extended business trip last week. He'd never gone on an extended business trip like this one before.

She tried to think about his arms wrapped around her in a hug, comforting her, telling her everything would be all right, that he wouldn't let anything happen to her. If only he were in the country. If only she'd gotten the chance to try and convince the man how she really felt about him. And it for damn certain wasn't as the little sister to his best friend.

Another set of hands grabbed her hips, pulling and tearing at her shorts. She felt the button pop and heard it drop to the ground in her heightened state of awareness.

An inhuman snarl erupted from Nikki's throat and with strength she didn't know she possessed, she shoved backward and jabbed her free elbow into her assailant's soft belly. He grunted in surprise, and she turned, facing them.

"Bitch," a second man hissed, backhanding her with a brutal swing of his arm.

Nikki stumbled, electric pain flaring across her mouth. The metallic taste of blood flooded her mouth. Beyond enraged, she raised her key-spiked hand and brought it down in a savage arc, raking it across the man's face. He howled in pain and jerked back a step, covering his face with both hands. The third man stood shocked beside his two degenerate friends.

She took the millisecond advantage and moved into flight mode.

Somehow Nikki managed to unlock her door and jump in before the three assholes knew what happened. One of them came to life and shouldered into the driver's door. The car shook as she punched down the lock with a fist.

Terror swept through her, lending to the adrenaline rush. Her hands were shaking hard and it took her three tries to get the key in the ignition.

Stupid!

Nikki laid on the horn as the engine roared to life. She twisted in her seat, looking back and forth for the men. Her breath heaved in and out, in sync with the wild hammer of her heart. She shifted into reverse and squealed out of the spot. Another quick check in the rearview mirror revealed nothing. The men had disappeared amidst the cars. They were still out there somewhere though, and they had to be angry.

Lightning forked across the sky, illuminating black clouds billowing on the horizon.

God, what should she do? Find a security guard in the mall, go to the station, call 9-1-1? Her hands shook uncontrollably as she tried to pull the phone out of the bag still draped around her shoulders. Finally she managed to dig it out. The antenna knob got stuck on something inside the bag.

"Damn it," she yelled, tears spilling down her cheeks, her nose running. She jerked and managed to extract it only to inadvertently throw it across the passenger seat. It clattered to the floor between the seat and the door.

A wild sob tore from her throat. She had to report this. Now, before they got away. She'd have to find a guard.

"No," she cried, wildly searching for the van again.

She would not get out of this Jeep to go in and look for a security guard. Fuck that. Wasn't about to happen. She could call them from home. All she wanted to do right now was take a shower and wash away the filth she felt crawling on her skin, seeping beneath until it mingled in her bloodstream, contaminating her to the very core.

Nikki took the turn onto the outer road almost on two wheels, narrowly missing an oncoming car.

"Where the hell were you a minute ago?" she screamed. Tears streamed down her face, mingling with the coppery blood at the corner of her lip. Her ponytail had come loose in the altercation. She swept an unsteady hand through the long dark mess and tucked it behind her ear. Instinctively, she grappled with the seat belt, barely getting it clicked in place.

The shakes took over from the tips of her fingers to the soles of her feet. She shouldn't be driving. At this rate she was likely to cause an accident. Nikki pressed harder on the accelerator. Putting distance between her and the mall was her number one priority.

Fifteen minutes later, she took the exit toward home. Except for the nervous glances in all of the mirrors every few seconds, she didn't remember driving the busy highway. Everything blurred in her mind.

The storm had picked up intensity, blowing leaves and trash in a whirlwind pattern across the two-lane highway she turned onto. Darkness had descended completely, lit up sporadically by the lightning. No matter. She could drive this stretch of lonely highway by rote, she'd done it so many thousands of times since turning sixteen. Not many people knew these back curving highways with hills to one side and short drop-offs to the other like she did.

She pursed her lips and moaned when the action pulled at the wound in the corner of her mouth. How in the hell would she explain her face to Derek when she got to their shared home? He'd be beyond livid.

Not to mention she had to somehow keep it from getting to Eli. The mere thought made her lightheaded. The man would flip, probably bunker down in protection mode and never let her out of the house again.

Like any big brother would.

Except Eli wasn't her big brother. Derek handled that particular role. In spades. He would flip too. And probably go on a murderous rampage with Eli in tow. No, Eli would be in the lead. If he were in the friggin' country, anyway.

"There. I won't have to tell him. He's not here." A sob burst from her pursed lips. She needed Eli. Needed to feel his fantastic arms around her, telling her, no, promising her, this would be all right. She was ready for him to comfort her as a woman and not a kid sister, and he was in some godforsaken country babysitting some kind of dignitary.

Who was she kidding? He'd never look at her or touch her again after this. She'd forever be the poor little almost raped victim. No. She wouldn't think that way. This was Eli, her brother's best friend, *her* friend. The more likely scenario would be for him to hunt them down and kill them with his overprotective macho demeanor.

Damn, just thinking Eli might look at her differently choked her.

Bright lights bounced off the rearview mirror, blinding and disorienting her. She groped for the tab on the mirror to adjust it.

The dark ribbon of highway with intermittent private drives and woods swallowed her car as it ate up the miles. Miles she gladly put between her and the mall she would never shop at again. Derek would have to call and tell the security there what happened, because she didn't even want to think about it anymore. She shivered. The sounds and smells returned with a vengeance. Just the thought of the garlic on that asshole's breath made her queasy. Another thing she'd do without for a long time.

The Jeep lurched forward with a bone-grinding crunch to the rear bumper, wrenching her neck. Nikki gripped the steering wheel and clenched her jaw, a thousand things running through her mind.

"What the hell?"

She searched the side mirror but saw nothing. What happened to the car behind her? Had it spun off the road after hitting her? A shadow emerged with another lightning strike, outlining a car so close she couldn't see the front end and either the headlights had gotten smashed or the driver had turned them off.

Nikki's stomach plummeted and she sped up to try and get away.

The Jeep took another hit from behind. Her head snapped forward, sending a bolt of pain down her spine. She automatically grabbed the back of her neck with her right hand and tried to steer with the other, her fingers grasping the wheel with a death grip. The tires slipped off the paved road and onto the loose gravel shoulder. Panicked, Nikki yelped and jerked the steering wheel back to the left, swinging wildly across both lanes of highway.

She screamed when the front driver's side made contact with the guardrail protecting cars coming too fast from the other direction around this particular curve. She knew a ditch ran along the other side, the side she should be on. Red-hot sparks jumped off the front fender, showering the windshield as a screeching, ear-piercing grind split the already turbulent night air.

"Please God, no one come around the curve, please God," she chanted.

With sweaty palms, she yanked the leather-wrapped wheel in the other direction.

She was going to die.

The ghost car smashed into the rear passenger's side as she overcorrected. She spun out of control like a tilt-a-whirl and slammed both feet on the brake. The wheels locked up and screamed as they flew across the blacktop. Her stomach bottomed out before reversing direction and threatening to spew. Nikki's strength was nothing compared to these few tons of metal.

When the driver's side left the pavement again, she was facing the wrong direction and the car rocked precariously on its side. She held her breath and prayed for any miracle but knew it was too late.

Everything seemed to happen in slow motion. A pair of headlights lit up, blinding her for a second time, and the Jeep pitched to the left. For a split second, Nikki felt weightless. The blood rushed to her head a moment before her skull slammed into the side window. Glass rained on her face, the droplets hot in their attack.

After that she felt nothing but a dizzying tumble, like she was in a dryer.

She opened her eyes and the world spun. It took long seconds to realize she wasn't still moving. All her weight was slumped toward the passenger side, so something had stopped them from turning over further.

Nikki blinked. Her eyelashes were sticky so she let them flutter closed. It was easier than holding them open while she took stock of all her parts. Her fingers were still locked around the steering wheel which seemed to be much closer to her than when she'd gotten into the car earlier. Her foot was trapped somehow and felt weird. Thankfully her seat belt had held and now dug into her collarbone, hip and belly with the crushing force of all her weight.

Her head got heavier and heavier. Something dripped in a steady cadence on the bare skin of her right arm. She struggled to open her eyes and see what it was.

Dark and glistening in the blitz of lights from the dashboard. Blood. It ran in a river off her chin, pooling in a crease of her shirt next to her elbow. Where was it coming from? Her head didn't hurt. Then again, neither did her foot or any other part of her body.

She lifted her head a fraction. Facing the highway, she could see the other vehicle sitting idly, mocking her with its twin beams filtering through the smoke and steam escaping from the Jeep's engine. It wasn't a car, but something bigger, like a truck. Or a *van*.

She blinked, or thought she did, because when she opened her eyes again, the vehicle was gone. Her neck failed to support her head any longer. She dropped her chin awkwardly to her chest. The interior lights flashed ominously. White noise filled her ears as the blackness surrounded her.

I love you, Eli.

CB80

It didn't look possible that she'd make it. Not with the severity of her injuries. At the very least she was looking at a long recovery. The woman by her side was another matter altogether.

She moved from his line of vision and he cursed his location. The supply closet gave him a perfect hidey-hole to spy on her but he could only see out the slim crack the slightly open door afforded him. One hand on the light switch, ready to flick it on should he need to in case someone walked in and wondered what he was doing, he kicked the mop bucket out of the way. If he leaned a tiny bit this way...opened it a millimeter more... Aah, there she was. Her ample breasts stretched the fabric of her T-shirt and she had more than enough hips to bring any man to his knees.

Any man except him. No woman would ever make a pussy out of him.

She lifted the injured woman's hand. Tears streamed down her face. His cock stirred, signaling him.

She'd just made his list. He stroked his growing erection through his pants and sighed. There were three before her. He'd never deviated from his plans, he wasn't about to start now.

But damn he itched to. He gripped the door handle until his knuckles hurt. Temptation threatened to smother him.

"Fuck." No. Straying now could spell disaster. He would stick to the way he'd always done things. Soon. She'd come up soon enough. For now he'd settle for finding out her name. The hunt was half the fun anyway.

He smiled and gave his cock one last tug. Tonight he'd give it more of the attention it deserved. And her face would be the one he jacked off to.

Sweet victory would be his.

Chapter Two

Nikki muttered a curse for letting her stupid phobia get the better of her and punched 9-1-1 into her cell phone. She would simply hold her thumb over the send button and walk quickly. Or look like the chicken shit she'd become and run.

The parking lot was dark due to the storm earlier in the evening knocking out power. The convenience store was running on a backup generator, but was otherwise open for business.

"Lots of cars, lots of places to hide."

She shivered, despite the heat and humidity being forced upon the St. Louis area. Another line of thunderstorms was bearing down on them from the west and the weatherman had forecast a real doozy of a night.

Nikki clenched the bag of goodies until her knuckles turned white. *It* had happened on a night just like this.

The insane fear gripped her mind in a punishing hold, keeping her frozen in her spot.

If her brother Derek hadn't had to back out on her at the last second, she wouldn't be in this predicament. Of course, if she could grow up and get over it, she wouldn't be in this predicament, either.

You'd think eight months would be long enough to get over the incident. Unconsciously, she reached up to the right side of her face and touched the thin, smooth scar that zigzagged from the corner of her eye to the bottom of her earlobe. Two plastic surgeries hadn't been able to completely get rid of it.

"Excuse me."

Nikki jumped at the terse female voice coming from behind and spun around, her heart pounding and her plastic grocery sack swinging in a wide arc.

"Sorry." She winced. The lady had to practically dive out of the way before Nikki's bag, filled with a two liter of Sprite and a box of Ho Hos, could take her legs out.

Follow her, be with somebody. Except, the lady was going in the opposite direction. And if her horrified gasp when she'd seen Nikki's face was anything to go by, she probably couldn't wait to get away from the crazy, maimed woman glued to her spot in the doorway.

Would she ever get used to people looking at her like she was a monster?

Nikki's shoulders drooped in resignation. Get it over with, go, go. She slid the plastic bag's handles onto her wrist and held the phone in that hand, her thumb at the ready. In the other hand she clutched the small can of pepper spray attached to her key chain.

She set a world-record pace and made it to her car without incident, shutting herself in and slamming her fist down on the automatic lock button. No more manually locked cars for her. Her lungs heaved with each breath, seizing up and threatening to shut off completely. A problem she'd dealt with since waking up in the hospital two days after her car had flipped.

With shaky fingers, she inserted the key and turned it.

Nothing.

"Fuck." The blood drained from her head, and her stomach dropped. "No, no, no. Damn it." Tears trickled down her face and her throat burned as the middle stages of a panic attack set in. "Please God, *please*, don't do this to me." A streak of lightning lit up the dark lot, followed instantaneously by a clap of thunder close enough that the hair on her arms and cheeks stood up. "Jesus!" She wiped at her running nose with a tissue from the console.

They were out there, watching. Waiting for her to drive, to be alone on an isolated road again. She could feel their hands closing over her mouth, moving down her body, pulling at the waistband of her shorts, a hardness digging into her thigh as they taunted her. It hadn't mattered that she'd gotten away, they'd jumped in their car and chased her down. Literally. Sometimes she swore she'd heard maniacal laughter as they sat there on the highway watching her life drain away.

"No!" Nikki ground the heels of her hands into her eye sockets. When would this end? Would she ever feel safe? Even when it had happened and she'd moved back home with her mom and dad, she hadn't felt safe. Their security and love hadn't been enough.

And Eli...well, she'd had to beg her parents and her brother Derek not to tell him. Not then, and not now. She'd loved him for too long, even if he didn't know it, and there was no way she wanted him to know about what those men had almost done to her.

What they *had* done to her face. Somehow she'd have to hide in plain sight when he came home in a few days because the pity she knew she would find lurking behind the golden brown depths of Eli's eyes would kill her. She didn't want his pity. He was a busy man, staying away from him might not be too hard.

And she lived in a delusional world.

Just thinking about him made her pussy tingle with heated desire. Unbelievable, considering the circumstances. Right after the attack happened, she believed she would never be able to stomach another man's touch. Instead, as the months went by she found more and more of her nights filled with erotic dreams. Of Eli. Dreams which were slowly taking the place of the nightmares, yet left her unsatisfied and wondering what it would be like if Eli ever touched her for real.

And there were still the rumors. Talk that he and his family were werewolves. Derek had never quite confirmed the possibility whenever she asked. That alone made her wonder if the rumors were really true. What she needed was a flat-out, laugh-in-her-face, "what the hell made you think that", type of solid, absolute "no" answer.

Instead, the one time she'd straight out asked her brother, he'd given her an exasperated sigh and turned his back on her like a recalcitrant child. Something about the calm, even tone of his voice when he said, "You seen your psychiatrist lately?" had put her senses on high alert. She'd been on the lookout for some kind of sign for the last few years, but nothing, nada. You'd think after all the years she'd known Eli, she would sense if he were somehow different from her.

Nikki snorted thinking about her psychiatrist. Lately even a few days were too long for her to wait between visits. Every miniscule noise seemed to freak her out. Maybe her increased anxiety had something to do with Eli returning home later this week.

She sniffed and wiped at the tears soaking her cheeks. A fat drop of rain splattered on her windshield. How appropriate.

She was late. Her friends were already at Lou's house, girls' night out party central, and were probably getting concerned.

About thirty minutes ago, she'd called Lou to let her know she was running a few minutes behind. When no one answered, she'd shrugged it off. They were home, she knew, having already talked to them earlier in the day to find out what kind of chips they wanted.

No way would she call again. Lou didn't need to know that Nikki had been too afraid to walk through a dark parking lot. She wanted to have fun tonight, relieve a little tension and not give her friends another reason to walk on eggshells around her.

She reached for the key again and the engine roared to life. A bark of laughter burst out of her mouth at her overwrought behavior. The four- door Civic zipped out of the parking spot when she stomped on the gas. With one more glance around her, Nikki put the car in drive and left the lot, only to come to a stop when the light at the next intersection turned red. A few more drops of rain fell heavily on her windshield and she tapped her fingers in agitation on the steering wheel, wondering if she would ever get over the feeling she was being watched.

The street wasn't busy. Most people were inside, out of the storm's path, but she had to grit her teeth against the eerie feeling worming its way through her body. Her tires squealed the second the light turned green.

Five minutes later she pulled up to the homey two-story house where Lou lived. Thank God the man Lou had been dating the last several months was gone on a business trip for the weekend. According to Amy and Kelly, he was kind of weird. Nikki didn't even know the guy's name. Jerry, Jim, Jake. Something starting with a "J". Of course, Nikki's attack made her opinion biased against most men so this guy would be no exception. If there had been even a hint he might show up tonight, she wouldn't have come in the first place since to this day, coming within ten feet of any man other than Derek or her father made her heart race. The mere thought of meeting a stranger tonight did not appeal.

Still, if she hadn't had the accident, Lou and this guy would never have met. It had been during one of the times Lou had visited Nikki at the hospital that they'd discovered each other and gotten close. Nikki didn't remember much from the weeks following the crash and Lou had seen enough of Nikki to know better than to introduce them. Hadn't stopped Lou from excitedly mentioning the man she was quickly falling in love with. She'd talked a few times about him. Nikki couldn't repeat much of what she'd heard because at the time, she'd pretty much blocked out any conversations involving men.

Nikki grabbed the bag of snacks and out of newly formed habit, palmed her can of mace. She raced up the walk and the two steps of the porch, shivering again at the tingle that crawled up the back of her neck. Music was blaring from inside and she smiled. The shits had started without her. Not that she was any kind of party girl, more so the pooper, but being with her friends always made her feel better. At least for the time she was with them. Tonight marked her first time attending their regularly scheduled girls' night out since the accident.

The front door was open.

Not wide open, just not latched as if whoever had closed it hadn't shut it all the way. A hard knock and the door would swing inward. Nikki shrugged, gave it a nudge with the toe of her tennis shoe and poked her head in, a false smile plastered on her face. Better to make them think she was okay after all this time.

Nikki knew something was wrong before she could even announce her arrival. The stench of blood gagged her, sending her stomach into a tirade. Bile squeezed into her throat. She wobbled in the doorway, frozen in time, and had to squelch the scream that bubbled up. They were dead. All of them. On the couch. Blood covered nearly every inch of what she could see through the wide opening above the half wall. Kelly's wide eyes stared unblinking at the ceiling. A gaping hole was the only thing left of what used to be her neck.

"Christ," she whispered raggedly, hoping against all hope she was having a nightmare.

A movement in the mirror hanging on the wall inside the door caught her attention. A dark head of hair and a set of wide shoulders dressed in black reflected back at her. He'd killed them! Mutilated them, and he was humming. An obscene tune that she somehow heard over the music as he ended one song and segued into a new one.

Call the police, get help. She shuffled back out the door, her heart in her throat, praying that the door wouldn't creak as she pulled it closed and reveal her. If any one of her friends was still alive, she had to help them.

A sob tore from her lips, sounding like a shotgun blast in the silent, humid calm before the storm. She winced and turned away, running back to her car. The bag of snacks fell off her wrist and landed with a thud on the porch, giving her away for sure.

Nikki slammed into the back bumper of her car with her thigh, and was thrown off balance. Her body twisted, her foot slipped on the wet pavement, and she went down hard. Her face scraped against the concrete when she wasn't able to catch herself, making her cheek burn.

"Son of a bitch!" The deep, angry voice rang out behind her.

There was a popping noise, once, twice. Nikki scrambled around the trunk of her car. A pinch pulled at the top of her shoulder. A heated whine filled the air next to her ear. He was shooting at her! Her heart hammered as she bent in half, using the car to shield her body.

With a yank, she opened the door and jumped in. The passenger side window exploded. Something plowed into the floorboard, burying itself in the carpet and out of sight.

She screamed and jammed the key into the ignition, stomping on the gas pedal at the same time. The tires squealed as they fought for purchase on the rain-slicked ground. Another bullet slapped against the dashboard. Sparks flew out of the area around the radio causing it to pop and hiss. Nikki screamed again and threw her arm up over her head, deflecting the sparks that leapt out at her.

The car shot forward, pounding her back into the seat. Glass shattered again as the rear window took a hit. Hunkered down, she sped off down the street, her screams echoing in the night.

CB&O

"Fucking cunt." He stomped through the house collecting his gear, hurried now that he'd been interrupted. No way would that whole scene not have attracted attention. The bitch had been screaming her head off. He'd used a silencer, but she'd made enough goddamn noise to wake the dead.

He'd hit her, he was sure. He wished it had been her head instead of her shoulder, he would have liked to see her skull explode. Too merciful for what she could potentially do to him, but extremely effective.

And where the fuck had she come from? For four months he'd been casing Lou, though he'd met her eight months ago. At first he'd set his sights only on her but had changed his mind after learning her pattern. Friday night parties for three. He'd envisioned taking all three of them as a challenge. In all the time he'd watched them he'd never fucking seen anyone else join them. He'd fucked up. Taken a drastic chance when he should have stuck to what he was comfortable with. But no. What had started out as a desire to have the woman he'd first seen eight months ago by her dying friend's side, had blossomed into his cock's demand for three women.

He'd studied them and had quickly learned the three were closer than close and he hadn't been able to resist.

"So again, where the *fuck* did you come from?"

The meddling bitch was one of the reasons he liked doing this. Fucking women couldn't keep their goddamn noses out of everyone else's business. He forced himself to stop and breathe. He had a few minutes. It would take a little while for people to come out of their houses and decide if what they'd heard had been real or not. There wasn't anything out there to see right now anyway. No one would equate the noises to this house.

He calmed himself enough to tune out the wailing of the radio, and listened to the final silence of death surrounding him. Tonight he'd done himself proud, taking out three cunts at once.

He'd been methodically cleaning up when he'd heard *her*. At a dead sprint, he'd hurdled the couch, coming inches from kicking one of the dead girls in the head. The only option left to him when he'd thrown open the front door was to shoot. She'd already gotten to her car, but had fallen, giving him an opportunity. He still couldn't believe he'd fucking missed.

No one would ruin this night for him. The adrenaline that had been fading just before his little witness had shown up was back with a vengeance. His dick hardened and his fingers itched to stroke himself. Even after all the fucking he'd done tonight, the damn thing wanted more.

He packed all of his things away, leaving absolutely no trace of himself behind. Twenty-three times he'd done this without getting caught. Tonight would be no different. He stripped out of his black sweatshirt and pants, groaning when his cock jumped against the waistband as he dragged it over his hips.

A good whore would fix his raging hard-on.

After changing into clothes that weren't spattered with blood, he took off into the night, via the back door. The police would be there soon and he had other things to do. Namely, finding the bitch who'd seen him.

Chapter Three

Eli Graham wrestled his suitcase from underneath two others as it tried to slither away from him on the carousel. Eight long, fucking months. More than eight months actually. Eight days more to be precise, not that he was counting or anything. You would think a man would have more than a couple of suitcases after having been away that long. But he was home now, and he wouldn't be leaving again.

Eight months was a lot of time to think about what he really wanted in life. And what he really wanted, what had been eating at him for nearly a year, was Nikki-Raine Taylor, his best friend's kid sister. A human.

His mate. He'd tried to deny what his body had been telling him for too long. Tried to protect her from who he really was instead of scaring her off with the truth. He couldn't do it anymore. Now that he was back, he was going to have her.

"Eli, you old dog. S'bout time you got back."

Eli grinned at the sound of his best friend Derek's voice and turned with a playful left hook at the ready. Derek dodged the blow and countered with one of his own, landing a punch on Eli's upper shoulder.

"Hey, man, how's it hanging?" Eli slapped one hand into his friend's and pounded him on the back with the other. Derek reciprocated. "It's been what, not more than twenty-four hours since we talked?"

They had talked on the phone every few weeks since Eli had left on a pack security assignment that had taken him out of the country for all of the eight months. It had been hard on him, when he was used to seeing his family and Derek's nearly every day. Then there was his nephew to think about, who could make an appearance any day even though Tieran still had something like two weeks left. To hear his sister-in-law tell it, she was ready to rip the poor kid out of her belly herself. Knowing her klutzy ways, if she tried, she'd end up on the floor on her ass. He smiled at the image.

"You ready?"

Eli didn't miss the gruff tone of Derek's question. He looked closely at the man who'd been more like a brother to him than a friend. There were dark circles under his bloodshot eyes and more than a day's worth of stubble on his face. Something was wrong.

"What is it?" Eli stood rigidly, his heart pounding. Please God, don't let it be Nikki-Raine. If something had happened to her while he was gone...

Derek swallowed, his jaw ticking, confirming Eli's suspicion that something bad had occurred.

"I'll tell you in the car." Derek's voice cracked. He bent over to pick up one of Eli's suitcases before turning his back on Eli and striding toward the exit.

Not good. This was not good.

Ten minutes later, they were sitting in Derek's SUV driving west on Highway 70, headed toward St. Charles county, where Derek's family and Eli's pack both lived.

"Don't keep me in suspense here, Der. What the hell is going on?" Eli settled his arm along the doorframe and turned in his seat to face Derek. The muscle was jumping once again along his jawline.

"It's Nikki. She's in big trouble, and we need your help." He glanced Eli's way, his eyes pleading. "You couldn't have gotten here at a better time."

Eli's heart stopped and he closed his eyes to ward off the pain swamping his chest.

"Is she sick?" He had to force the words out of his mouth, scared to death that Derek would say yes. That he wouldn't have the chance to claim her as his mate before she was gone.

Derek shook his head. "No. Worse." Derek maneuvered the car onto the Rock Road exit lane, then parked in a lot not far from the highway. "She witnessed a murder last night. The killer got away."

Eli exploded. "Why the fuck didn't you call me?" His wolf rippled through him, fighting its way to the surface, ready to rip apart the man who'd dared draw his mate into a violent situation.

"And what the fuck were you going to do?" Derek shouted. "You were halfway around the goddamn world, probably already packing to get on a plane. You couldn't have gotten here any sooner." He drew in a sharp breath and gripped the steering wheel until his knuckles turned white.

"Where is she?" Eli rasped, aware that yelling at each other was not going to get anything accomplished. He clenched his hand into a fist and fought the urge to punch something.

"The hospital." Derek's answer was just as grim as his face had been earlier.

Eli whipped his head up. "What for?"

"She was shot trying to get away from the sick fuck. Not bad, more like a scrape, but they kept her overnight."

Eli wrenched the door open and stumbled out, puking on the ground before he could get two steps. He'd been out pulling babysitting duty half a world away to a goddamn werewolf dignitary, and Nikki was here getting shot. Just the thought of what a bullet would do to her tender flesh had him heaving again. A monumental battle ensued inside him between his wolf's need to protect his mate and his human's need for revenge.

Derek's shadow fell over him.

"That was not the reaction I was expecting. You want me to break your nose now, or wait 'til you're out of your misery?"

Eli straightened. "What the hell are you talking about?"

"Oh, come on. She's my baby sister, my only sister, but I didn't puke my guts out when I heard what happened."

"Back off, Der. You don't know what you're talking about," he growled.

"You been with her?"

Derek was obviously itching for a fight. Eli wasn't going to give him the satisfaction. "No, but if I had been, it wouldn't be any of your business."

The fist caught him just below the eye. Eli took it, the momentum dragging him to one side, but otherwise, he stood his ground. Derek hopped around, shaking his hand out. When he stopped, he propped his hands on his hips and cocked his head to one side, leaving Eli feeling like a bug under a microscope.

Long seconds passed until both men caught their breath. Eli's cheek throbbed, letting him know that within minutes he'd have a shiner.

"You love her? Did you"—he waved his hand in a circle—"mate her or whatever it is you do?" Derek asked.

Eli contemplated what to say. How could he tell his best friend he loved his sister and wanted to do all kinds of things to her delicious little body? He couldn't.

Eli nodded. "She is my mate, but no, I haven't claimed her. I was planning on doing that when I got back here." He turned and climbed into the SUV.

Derek followed suit, sliding into the driver's seat and taking off toward 70 again.

"How long have you known, E?" Derek demanded softly.

Eli sensed a good amount of pain coming from his best friend. "About a year."

"Why the hell didn't you tell me?"

"What did you want me to say? Excuse me, my wolf has just announced that it's found its mate, and guess who it is?"

"You fucking hurt her…"

"I won't."

"What about Caelan? Does he know? Is he good with little brother taking a mate?"

What the hell was going on here? He'd never seen Derek act like this before. Granted, Eli had never told his best friend he wanted Nikki for a mate, but he also never thought Derek would be anything but happy for them both.

"Are you trying to justify me being with your sister or something?"

"No. Yes." He pounded the steering wheel with his fist. "I don't know. Son of a bitch. It's just that…she's not gonna take this well right now. Caelan knows it. I wondered if he'd tried to talk you out of it or something."

"What does Caelan know?" Eli growled.

Derek shrugged. "I called him. He knows what's going on. Nikki's not really comfortable around men any... Shit." Derek slapped at the steering wheel again, clearly frustrated.

He wasn't the only one.

"Not comfortable with men?" Since when was Nikki Taylor not comfortable with men? Most of the time she played better with the boys than the girls. Had been that way for as long as Eli had known her. She'd take a T-shirt and jeans over dresses any day. For her, nice clothes were reserved for church, sometimes not even then, and weddings or funerals.

"I didn't mean it that way," Derek fudged.

"What the hell has gotten into you? Caelan has no say in who I mate with. *I* don't even have control. Jesus, just ask him about finding his mate. When he met Tieran, we were hunting that killer, remember? She had a vision and thought it was *me* killing those women. Did you forget about my being arrested and conked over the head, and framed for the murders? If you were married, would you leave your wife if she'd been the one to put your brother in jail? No. You wouldn't and Caelan didn't either, because as a mate, he physically can't. It would kill him." Eli rubbed a hand over his face and tried to pull back on the escalating shouting. "Like it will me, once I've claimed Nikki as my own.

"We're men too, Derek," Eli continued, calmer now. "Each of us takes a mate whether we're head alpha or not. We just don't get to choose who our woman will be, some sick twist of fate does." He grunted. "Fate happened to bring me Nikki, and I couldn't be prouder or happier. She might not take to the whole idea right away, but once it's done, it's done. We're one soul for life. Sooner or later she'll figure that out, and you fucking know all this, Der, so why the questions?"

"Some shit happened... I'm not supposed to say anything to you. I promised her I wouldn't."

Eli sat up. Suddenly they were keeping secrets from each other? "Don't start something you can't finish. If something happened I need to know about, you better get your ass talking. I don't care if she made you swear on your grandmother's grave." This day just kept getting worse and worse. Instead of coming home and seeing Nikki-Raine's beautiful smile for the first time in eight months, Derek kept dropping ugly little bombs.

What could be worse than getting fucking shot at by a murderer? Ominous dread crept along his spine.

"She was..."

"She was what?" Eli gritted out when Derek took too long to finish.

"Attacked, all right? She was attacked one night as she walked to her car."

"When and how?" he asked with deadly calm. Attacked could mean a lot of things. Someone could have written on her forehead with a blue marker, she could have been bitten by a dog, mugged or...

Derek's sigh filled the car, deep with resignation. "Right after you left. Some dickheads cornered her in a parking lot—"

"Pull over. Now!"

He did, slamming on the brakes and sliding to a stop on the shoulder.

Eli drove his fist into Derek's unsuspecting chin. "Goddamn it." He shook his hand, testing the already bruising knuckles by bending them, and fighting to keep his wolf in check.

"Son of a bitch." Derek groaned beside him. Now they had both taken their potshots and could get on with their lives.

"I'm not even going to ask what your excuse was for not calling me eight months ago, just tell me what the fuck happened."

"I can't tell you much."

"Tell me, or so help me God…"

"That's just it. I can't. Three men accosted her as she walked to her car from the mall. They tried to force her to the ground. Somehow she got away, but they followed her car and ran her off the road. We think."

"You think?" Eli hissed.

Derek looked him straight in the eye. "There's no tangible evidence it was the same car she'd seen the men next to in the lot. It was dark and she couldn't see well and afterward she had a hard time remembering anything about the accident itself. Her injuries were serious. She had to have a few surgeries that didn't completely fix what was broken and she's terrified of seeing you. That's all I know. That and the fact she changed after it happened. Moved back in with Mom and Dad, doesn't go out much at night unless she has to, or date."

Thank God for that. At the moment, Eli was likely to kill any man who got within fifty feet of her.

"Was she raped?" he rasped. If she'd been fucking raped, and he hadn't been here to prevent it… But terrified of seeing him? Why? What the hell did she think he'd do? Reject her? Inconceivable.

"When the police hit a roadblock, I immediately went to Caelan. Against her wishes, E. She begged Caelan not to tell you, like she begged me. Caelan very reluctantly agreed. At the time, I think he could see how scared she was about seeing you and there was no reason to upset her even more. We did everything possible to find out who did it, but ended up with nothing. You couldn't have done anything different. It still would have happened."

Derek spoke softly, and had apparently learned to read minds while Eli was away. He must have been talking to Eli's psychic sister-in-law lately. He ground his teeth until his jaw hurt. Derek was right, it probably still would have happened. But at least if he had been here, he could have helped get her back on her feet. And taken the bastards out as only a shifter could.

Except, if Caelan hadn't been able to find them there was a good chance he wouldn't have been able to either. His brother was one of the best trackers around, despite being duped by that murdering son of a bitch traitor of a shifter a while back.

Eli swiped his hands down his face, ignoring the throbbing in both his knuckles and his cheek.

"At least now I know why she didn't want to tell you."

"What do you mean?" Eli jerked his gaze up. He had no clue what Derek was talking about.

"Are you that dense? She loves you."

Chapter Four

Nikki tried to sleep, she really did, it just wasn't happening. The bed was too hard, the pillow too starchy, her shoulder burned like hell and she had to lie on her bad side. The one she'd never been able to sleep on, but had to now because she'd been shot on her good side. Skinned anyway. She'd hate to know what it felt like to actually be shot.

Shot. A murderer had shot at her because she'd seen him. Thank God it had only been a flesh wound. What he'd done to her friends was unconscionable. And he was still out there. Looking for her, if the police were correct in their assumption. Nikki sniffled and gripped the blanket tighter around her chin, knowing it wouldn't protect her from the man who'd tried to put a bullet through her head.

All night long she'd cried about the senseless waste of the lives of her friends. It didn't matter that she hadn't been around much in the better part of the last year. At one time they'd all been very close. Now they were gone and she'd never see them again. Would she ever see anything past the horrific end of their lives? A sob stuck in her throat, choking her, but no tears came. There weren't any tears left to cry.

Derek had stayed through the night, staking himself out in front of the door, cracking his knuckles and frowning at anyone who opened it. As if the man would try to get at her here. As if

Derek would be able to stop another bullet meant for her. They'd both be dead and it would be all her fault.

This morning her dad had shown up again and relieved her brother. The police followed shortly thereafter, asking another round of a bazillion questions, most of which she couldn't answer. Still. Things hadn't changed any since she'd gone through them last night. The most she'd had to offer had been what she'd seen of the killer's dark hair in the mirror and what her friends had said about Lou's weirdo boyfriend. Since she'd never met the man, no, she couldn't give them a description, much less a name. And no too, to the question did she think he could have done this? She had no idea. Didn't they get that she didn't know him?

Not only that, but her brain was fried from whatever the doctor had given her so she couldn't think straight. She thought it had been something for anxiety. Or pain, maybe. Both, more likely. Last night she'd been a complete basket case and she'd welcomed anything that might soften the blow of what had happened.

Today she was marginally clearer and had a vague recollection of a conversation she'd had with Lou in the hospital all those many months ago. Lou had talked about her boyfriend and how sometimes he seemed like he was far away. As if he were lost in thought or something. Lou had seemed genuinely happy with him though, and he certainly didn't seem to put too much pressure on her.

What kind of help would those shady, drug-hazed memories be anyway? She'd spent a long time in the hospital when Lou had met him. After leaving, Nikki had sort of shut herself off. Hidden would be the best word, like a coward. She should have stayed in hiding so she wouldn't have seen the gruesome—

Stop! Nikki slammed the door on the direction her brain was going. Reliving it did nothing but bring on the tears. She just wanted to sleep. To forget about what had happened for a few blessed minutes. But had she been able to do that yet? No.

When the police had finally left, her mother had asked her pastor to stop by, so she'd cried again, all the while being patted and told that it was all in God's master plan. Right now, what she really wanted was to tell God just where he could shove his master plan, because it sucked. When the patronizing pastor had finally left, exhaustion set in.

"Hey, Nikki-Raine."

Oh God. No. No, no, no. No one called her Nikki-Raine but him. Why, God? Was it because I told you what you could do with your plan? Please tell me I'm hallucinating the deep voice behind me. Please! She squeezed her eyes shut. He could not see her right now, ever, and damn it, where had he come from anyway? Wasn't he supposed to be off guarding some head of state or something? He couldn't be here. Not now.

"You awake, baby?"

Baby? He'd never called her baby before. His big hand, callused she knew, rubbed a path down her blanket-covered leg from knee to ankle. Nikki froze and held her breath. He'd never touched her this way before, either. Her pussy flooded, creaming her panties, and her tummy jumped. She jerked at her body's response. How could she feel this way right now? Right when the world was wrong? How could anything feel this right? At any rate it made her blessedly forget the physical and emotional pain she was in, if only for a few seconds.

Do it again, she begged silently. Just once more. If this was all she could get from the man she loved, she'd take it.

He did. A tender stroke that had her swallowing back a wave of fresh emotions that threatened to choke her.

"What are you doing here?" She forced the words around the pain.

He chuckled once, the sound slamming through her system, making her whole body jerk with the deep baritone. "Your mom hired me. I talked to her after Derek picked me up from the airport."

Hired you for what? Personal security, his business, you idiot, what else. That's why he was here. To babysit her. The bed dipped behind her butt, unbalancing her just enough that she had to tighten her already crushing hold on the blanket to keep from rolling to her side. Not only would her shoulder burn like hell, but he'd also see her face.

And probably leave.

"And we need to talk." His hand stopped tracing her calf muscle and gave it a squeeze instead. "But first, you need to get up so we can get you out of here. It isn't safe." He started to stand, still holding her leg.

No way was she leaving here with the one man who could destroy her, shattering her heart into little bits with one look.

"Uh-uh."

His hand tightened around her calf and she winced.

"Excuse me?" His tone reeked of disbelief, reminding her of all the times he'd talked to her as a child, back when she'd been a pest to him and her brother. "Goddamn it, look at me, Nikki-Raine."

She sighed. She hated it when he used that nickname. He was the only one who did, and he never made it sound like she dreamed it should. Like a man who wanted to jump into bed with her. Or on the floor, or against the wall, or the table. She wanted to try all those things. With him. Eight months ago she might have still had a chance. Now she no longer had that option.

Why wouldn't she look at him? He'd known her her whole life, had seen her at her worst, and now suddenly she didn't want him to see her? Hell, at her senior prom, he'd nearly ripped the fucking head off her date, who'd decided to leave with another girl. She'd run from the hotel, mortified and sobbing, and called home for someone to pick her up. Derek and Eli had been there playing pool and had driven off to get her before even hanging up the phone.

When she'd run to Derek as he stepped out of the car, her face red, her nose running and her eyes puffy from crying, Eli had wanted to intercept her and take her into *his* arms. *He* wanted to be the one to console her and it had taken all his willpower not to. Not with him being twenty-three and her just eighteen. Jailbait. At least that's how he'd thought of her at the time. She might have been legal but something had felt wrong about it. Not to mention the fact he was a shape-shifter, something he'd always thought would repulse her.

Then there'd been the time when her appendix had almost ruptured. He'd seen her just after the surgery. For weeks she hadn't looked herself, but was still more than beautiful to him.

If he could just get her the hell out of here, he might be able to explain some of that to her.

She had the fucking blanket wrapped so tight around her, it was a wonder she hadn't strangled herself to death yet. He grabbed a handful near her slim hip, and gave a yank.

She hissed in pain as the fabric pulled at her shoulder. "Christ. I'm sorry, Nikki-Raine." He leaned over her, hovering just above where the fucker had shot her, and looked into her face. It was all scrunched up, her eyes squished closed, her teeth biting into her bottom lip. "Damn it, baby." He rested his hand on her upper arm and tried to soothe her. Scratch or not, she'd been shot. It had to hurt. Causing her more pain wasn't in the cards.

"Please...just go." Her broken whisper ripped a hole in his chest, making it difficult for him to breathe.

"No way in hell, Nik. If I have to carry you out of this hospital, I will."

"No," she sobbed, burying her head deeper into her pillow.

Eli sighed. He should have known this wasn't going to be easy. Hell, Derek had warned him that she wouldn't want anything to do with a man, especially not after the things she'd seen the night before. But, damn it, he wasn't just some run-of-the-mill man. He had years of training in this kind of stuff, co-owned a personal security company with his brother. If there was one thing he knew, it was how to keep a person safe.

Safe from the bad guys, not from him, because she was about to learn how much the wolf and the man in him wanted her, no matter what had happened in the past.

"Nikki, they aired a segment on the news last night and this morning. He knows you're out here, honey. Fuck, barring that he's a complete idiot, which is highly unlikely, he knows you're at *this* fucking hospital." A subject which his brother, Caelan, was broaching right now with the local police out in the hall. The bastards couldn't have put out a bigger ad as to where their witness was.

"Then I'll go with my parents." Her voice was muffled against her pillow, aggravating the shit out of him. She almost seemed shy.

Fine, if she wouldn't come to him, he'd go to her.

"I know about what happened, Nikki-Raine." He slid his hand along the crook of her arm and tore the blanket from her tight little fist, covering it with his own, feeling her out-of-control pulse along her wrist as he did so.

Just as he thought. She was scared to death. Not only of the killer, but him. His throat burned when she tried to curl into a tighter ball under him. The way he had her pinned beneath his armpit only curved her more fully into his chest and arm so that he was essentially holding her, cradling her body with his own.

"Like you said, it was just on the news." She sniffed again and with his thumb, he flicked a tear off the only side of her nose he could see, not letting go of the hand he held.

He pushed at the stray wisps of her beautiful, usually glossy, black hair and tucked them behind her ear. Leaning closer to her ear, careful not to touch her shoulder, he whispered to her, "I know about everything, sweetheart."

Her body went rigid, her breathing stopped. And then she cried, hiding her face even more, while he continued stroking her hair back from her sweaty face and caressing her fist with his thumb.

He would not give her a chance to back away from him, not even as her soulful sobs tried to squeeze the life from him.

"I know, and I don't care." It wouldn't bother him if her arms and legs were rearranged. He certainly wasn't going to be concerned about a scar on her cheek. Hell, he had his own share of scars.

Eli kissed her ear, smiling as he licked the lobe. She shivered and sniffed but at least stopped crying. He moved on to her shoulder, kissing gently along the bandages peeking out from beneath the blue floral print hospital gown. Then he levered himself up on the bed with one knee so he could lean more fully over her without hurting her.

His lips traveled up her shoulder into the sweet curve of her neck, which she granted him access to, along the curve of her jaw, and up to the corner of her mouth. Eli teased her lips with his tongue, and then licked along the path a tear had cut across her cheek, before adding a last kiss to her eyelid. She smelled so damn good.

Beneath his jeans, his cock hardened. If he didn't get off of her, he would do something stupid like roll her onto her back and flip that flimsy gown over her head so he could touch and sip at her small breasts. It was fucking hell imagining what color her sweet nipples would be, and how much of them he'd be able to get in his mouth.

They'd taste like ripe berries. He'd drown in them, sucking them strongly along his tongue and biting at them until she arched her back and begged him to touch her some more. And then he'd mark her skin with his teeth, announcing to every pack in the world who she belonged to.

Fuck. Fuck! He had to stop kissing her. Had to get her the fuck home where she'd be safe and he could ease her into his world. Having Tieran in the house would help, he hoped. His sister-in-law would at least be able to share her experiences as a somewhat new mate.

What was he doing to her? Her heart beat so hard he had to feel it clear through her back. His lips sent tiny electrical pulses zipping across her body. Without realizing what she was doing, Nikki lifted her head so he had better access. They had to stop before Derek came barging in and found his best friend smothering his little sister. With kisses.

"Stop, you have to..." She tilted her head an inch further but kept her eyes closed, afraid that if she opened them, he would disappear. "Right there. Oh God." She bit into her already punished lip. He was killing her.

Suddenly he was gone. His weight lifted completely off her, leaving her empty and mortified. She'd given in too easily and now he was backing off. He was probably disgusted with her.

"Your mom sent some clothes for you, sweetheart. Do you need some help getting them on?"

Oh right, like that's gonna happen, her mind said. Her pussy begged just the opposite. *Yes, rip off my clothes and take me.*

"I'm not a child, Eli." That's it, duck behind a cool demeanor like his kisses meant nothing to her. Anything to get him to leave her alone to wallow in her misery, before he saw her face.

"No, I can see that you're definitely not a little girl anymore." His voice was funny, like he was choking on his words.

Regretting that he'd ever touched her?

"Can you leave then?"

"I'll be outside the door. Caelan's here too. He's gonna help get you out of here without being seen. But understand this. I won't be leaving your side until this is over, so whatever freaky-deek notion you've got going on in that head of yours about not wanting to look at me, you better get over it pretty damn quick."

"Fine." She flung herself to a sitting position and, ignoring the ripping pain that tore through her shoulder, let her legs dangle over the edge of the bed. "Is this what you want?" she demanded. "You want to see what happens to a person's face when their car rolls over three or four times? Are you happy now?"

Her face was hot with her anger, the slash probably glowing against her red cheeks. Eli stood about five feet away, staring at her like she'd grown another head, his jaw ticking. Served him right. Maybe now he'd get over this ridiculous idea of kissing

45

her like she suddenly meant something more to him than just being Derek's sister.

His feet moved, stepping closer and closer to her. She couldn't look him in the eye anymore. Instead she focused on his scuffed, leather work boots. He didn't stop until his thighs touched her knees. His muscles rippled beneath his jeans as he took on a relaxed stance.

"Look at me."

She shivered and shook her head, allowing her long hair to fall forward and cover her face. Taking a deep breath, Nikki let her gaze wander up from where their legs touched and got caught on the way by the massive bulge just beneath his zipper. Swallowing was hard and her lips were suddenly dry.

"Look at me," he commanded her again.

"I am." Her words were whisper soft as she fixated on his cock and imagined what it would look like if she unzipped him and let it out.

"My face, sweetheart." He tilted her chin up with one long finger until her eyes met his. "As much as I'd love for you to get to know me that way, this isn't the time or place."

The cocky bastard was smiling. His brown eyes, yellowed with intensity, were crinkled at the corners and she got lost in their depths. Just below one eye was a hint of a forming bruise. Her heart lurched. Somehow he'd been hurt. His thumb came up to stroke her chin, making her completely forget everything except what his touch did to her.

"You're beautiful, sexy, smart, and I can't wait to bury myself inside your soft little pussy."

Nikki gasped. She squeezed her legs together and tried to stave off the impulses spiraling through her because of his words. He could not have just said that. Could he?

"Yes, I did, and we will. At home, where I can lock you away until I have uncovered every inch of your delectable body." Her heart pounded against her chest wall, her clit throbbing right along with it. "And then I'm going to taste everything I've just discovered."

"Oh my God." The starchy hospital gown rasped her nipples, making her moan and squirm.

"Now, get off that bed and get dressed so we can get the hell out of here."

Eli turned and walked out of the room, leaving her dazed. Never, in all the years she'd known him, had he ever talked to her the way he just had. Her arms and legs felt like mush and she was lightheaded.

She was dreaming. It had to be a dream. In a minute she would wake up and find Derek standing guard. Then she could chalk the whole Eli dream thing up to an erotic fantasy and forget it, because no way could she tell Derek about the thoughts she'd done so well in hiding about Eli for the last ten years.

"Get a move on, sis. Loverboy won't wait long."

Nikki jerked her gaze toward the door where Derek stood poking his head in and slapping the doorframe.

"How did..."

He walked over to her. "I had to tell him, Nik. His head nearly exploded when I told him about the killer. It made me do some thinking. And some punching," he admitted in a sheepish tone, his shoulders hunched like he was steering off a cold wind.

"So that's what happened to his cheek?"

Derek moved his jaw back and forth, a pained look on his face. "Yeah. I told him I'd kill him if he hurt you." He held up his hand when she would have spoken. "And there are things you don't know about him. Things he does that..." He stabbed his fingers through his hair. "Jesus. I can't believe I'm having this conversation with my little sister. Remember those times..."

"He's a werewolf?" Was she finally going to get her answer after all this time? There wasn't much that would stop her from being with Eli, but shifting into an animal form? She honestly didn't know how she felt about something that went well beyond the realm of possibility. Then again, Eli's sister-in-law could see things before they happened.

"You've known all along, haven't you? Who the fuck told you?"

Nikki laid her hand on his forearm. "Rumors, Derek, just rumors. And there are plenty of them circulating about Eli and his brother." His very gorgeous, identical twin brother, Caelan, who was apparently here somewhere. "You certainly didn't help out any, never giving me a straight answer when I asked about them."

Her laugh quickly turned into a groan when a pain shot up her neck.

"Damn, sorry. The doc's on his way in to release you. Maybe he'll give you something for the pain."

She nodded, gritting her teeth, her lips pursed.

"Anyway, please do whatever Eli tells you to. He knows what he's doing."

Nikki's left eyebrow rose sharply. "Anything?"

Derek grunted.

Chapter Five

They were swarming like bees on honey. He stopped at the nurses' station down the hall and watched the small crowd gathered outside room 4112. The bitch's room. He eyeballed the whiteboard covered wall, found her room number and immediately had access to her name and condition.

Nicole Taylor, GSW, discharged. Son of a bitch. He slapped his hand down on the counter. The nurse jumped with a squeak and looked at him distractedly. He smiled at her until she smiled back. *Yeah, smile, you pretty little cunt. Forget I was here.* "Sorry," he said, making sure the charm dripped off the word.

"No problem." Two dimples appeared on her cheeks.

Fucking clueless woman.

There was a hallway between him and the group. He would only get as close as that. An older man, two younger men—identical muscle—and a uniform. The door was open so there was no telling how many other people were inside the room. Or how long the doctor would be before he let the bitch walk out the door.

He'd wait her out.

Then he'd finish what he'd started and kill her. It wouldn't be as sweet as fucking her first then ripping her apart with his bare hands, but he didn't have that luxury anymore.

CZ80

"What are we waiting for?" Nikki whispered, sandwiched between Caelan in front of her and Eli behind her. Caelan was so close, her arm, which she held carefully across her belly to lessen the tension on her shoulder, rode snugly along his muscle-bound waistline. She fought the urge to spread her fingers and cop a feel of his butt cheek and wondered if Eli's would feel the same. She giggled.

Eli's entire body was pressed up against her, his hard-on wedged firmly in the small of her back, making her squirm. She licked her lips, frustrated by the fact that she was turned-on at the most inopportune time by not only the man who had her heart but by his brother also. How Eli could have a boner right now, was anybody's guess.

He had both of her upper arms in his grasp, and for that she could kiss him. Every minute that went by, her body got heavier, her head lighter. Whatever the doctor had given her was working.

She leaned her head around Caelan's wide shoulders and looked out the double doors that led to the parking lot. Caelan's SUV was parked not more than twenty feet away, Derek standing guard like a sentry.

"Stand up," Eli hissed behind her and yanked her back upright. She felt nothing, not even a twinge in her shoulder.

"Geez." She yawned. "I was just wondering if you thought your big truck was gonna sprout wings and fly over here."

Caelan snorted. Her brain was getting foggier and her neck was starting to feel like a wet noodle. "I just need a little snooze." She yawned again and let her head fall forward to rest on Caelan's back.

"Uh-uh, not yet, sweet cheeks." Cealan stepped forward, turned and caught her head against his chest before it could fall off and roll on the floor. "Hey, Nikki." He snapped his fingers.

She giggled again.

"Oh brother. We're gonna lose her before we get her in the car."

"You guys are so cute."

Caelan pushed her head back with a thumb under her chin and laughed. "And you are stoned out of your mind."

Nikki reached out with her good hand and laid it on Caelan's chest. A deep growl reverberated down her spine. She thought the sound originated from Eli, but what kind of man could make that noise?

A werewolf.

Caelan cleared his throat. "It's not me you should be touching, sweetheart."

"But you look just like him," she sighed.

"Him is standing behind you and unless you get your hands off my brother, *him* is going to spank your little ass." Eli's big hand appeared and snatched hers off Caelan. He squeezed her fingers and tucked them behind her back, keeping them hostage.

"Poo. You're no fun," she pouted.

"When we get home, I'll show you all kinds of fun." Eli's warm, sultry words tickled her ear and her knees threatened to buckle with the insinuation. Even through the haze of drugs her body responded to him.

Caelan snorted and turned around again. Nikki shrugged her good shoulder and let her head fall forward once more. His back shook with laughter.

cઠ8౦

He whistled softly, his eye pressed to the scope of the rifle he'd procured from a secret compartment in his car. It was a special rifle. One he could carry in a gym bag and assemble and disassemble quickly without anyone knowing he had it on his person. He waited for the cunt to clear the double set of doors. If her leaving was supposed to be some clandestine mission, it wasn't working very well. Right now, Nicole Taylor was standing between the two hired muscles he'd seen outside her room. The front man turned and caught the woman who fell forward into him. She'd obviously been given some kind of sedating painkiller before her discharge.

Good, he'd have a better shot if they were moving slower. He swept the scope to the SUV parked at the curb. Another man stood on the rear passenger side, his hand on the door handle. Any second now, they'd escort Nicole out the door and into the waiting SUV. Then she'd be whisked away and much harder to find.

He could find her, he wasn't worried about that, but he didn't want to. He wanted her gone now. And he'd be conveniently missing whenever they found this little hidey-hole.

The first set of doors finally slid open and the trio stepped through.

"Yes, yes, come on." His finger tightened on the trigger. "Not yet." He took a deep breath.

The second set of doors opened.

"There you are." He tightened his finger again. He'd have a perfect opportunity when all three of them were out the door.

"Fuck!" A beam of sunlight reflected off a side swinging door when someone exited next to his witness, blinding him through the magnifying effects of the scope. He tore the rifle off his face and rubbed at his eyelids with his thumb and forefinger, desperately trying to ward off the sudden blindness before he missed his chance.

"Goddamn it!" By the time he was able to reposition himself, his prey was already at the car and one of the muscles was lifting her into the backseat. Then the man climbed in after her.

"Like a fucking sheet of glass is gonna keep your head from exploding." He could still do this. If the fucking man would get out of the way. He couldn't afford to take two shots. His palms sweated, making the rifle slick, and his heart rate fluctuated. "Bitch."

No woman was going to make him feel like this.

CB&O

Her slim body felt perfect in his, making him remember the time when she'd been sixteen and he'd had to drag her out of the lake when she'd gotten a cramp. Back then he hadn't thought anything of holding her so close. Now his cock hardened and begged his big brain for permission to bury itself inside her sweetness.

"You're my hero."

Her nasally rendition made Eli chuckle. Whatever that doc had given her was making her more than loopy. When she'd had her hand on Caelan, he'd just about lost it. Her hands weren't going to be touching anybody but him. Eli willed his erection away and sighed. She sagged in the seat, wilting even as he held her. Lifting and maneuvering her into the seat had been the easy part. Leaving the sweet vee of her thighs would be next to impossible. Nikki-Raine looked up at him, her eyes big, her lashes incredibly long and thick. His gaze drifted down to her tiny bow of a mouth just as the tip of her pink tongue darted out and swept across her bottom lip. He wondered what it would feel like wrapped around the head of his cock. Tight and wet and sucking him until every last drop of his come was wrung from his balls.

Jesus. There was going to be a fucking zipper line etched into his cock if she didn't stop tempting him. He tore his gaze back to the widened disks of her eyes. Her pupils were dilated and as much as he'd like to think it was because she felt the same way about him that he did about her, he knew it was whatever she was doped up on.

She blinked and squirmed her hips beneath his, rubbing along his cock inadvertently. Her eyes widened further in reaction to what she felt, and he couldn't resist.

Ever so slowly, as if they had all the time in the world, he lowered his head. "Turn your head now if you don't want this, Nikki-Raine, because once my lips touch yours, there's no turning back. You will be mine." His chest rumbled with his growl.

She shook her head and swallowed. "No."

Shock froze him in place. No? Fuck. His lungs bellowed as he forced air out of his clenched throat and closed his eyes.

A soft hand brushed his cheek, cupping his face. He opened his eyes.

"Please don't stop." She looked tormented, like a woman unable to get to her last meal.

He descended once more. His lips met hers, melding and sealing their mouths together. He licked along her perfect teeth until she opened for him, inviting him into the warm recesses of her mouth. Cinnamon burst on his tongue from her earlier gum chewing.

They dueled inside her mouth and he slanted his head. Deeper, he had to go deeper, to taste all of her. Nothing existed except the two of them.

Until Caelan cleared his throat and Derek pounded on the window.

Eli jerked his head away so fast he smacked the roof of the SUV, and glared at Nikki's mouth, now red and puffy. They were both breathing hard, panting. He lifted himself, or would have had his shirt not been twisted up in Nikki's fist.

"Later, baby. This isn't over. Not by a long shot." He dislodged her hand. "Trust me, when we get home, nothing will stop me from having you."

"But—"

"Nothing."

Her lips, still wet from his kiss, formed an "O". A perfect spot for his... Christ. Get it fucking together. His canines lengthened for the umpteenth time that day. He wanted to howl at the moon for the unfairness life had dumped at their feet.

He was supposed to have returned home, staked his claim and settled them at the ranch to raise the next generation of the pack. Instead he found himself having to delay his union and protect his mate from the vile life forms who'd dared to lay a hand on her sweet skin. He'd run every one of them to ground and tear them to shreds.

Nikki's eyes closed on a sigh and she slumped in the seat, resting her head on the armrest of the opposite door. Eli backed out of the car and shut the door.

Sucking in a deep breath, he faced his best friend and brother.

"You're good to go," Derek said. "I've been by the car since Caelan went in to get you. There's been nothing suspicious."

"Doesn't mean there's no one out there somewhere," Eli snarled, scanning the parking lot. Damn his hormones and lack of willpower. He should have had them out of here by now, instead of practically trying to mate with her in the backseat. Any other day, any other situation and he would have been long gone. Instead, he'd given anyone a chance to get to her.

Derek nodded. "You're right. And I'm trusting you to keep my baby sister safe." Derek backed away from the car.

"I will." He'd keep her safe or die trying. No one would take his mate now that he'd acknowledged her. And God help those who'd already tried.

"I'll call you later tonight." Derek turned and stalked off to his car.

"Let's get out of here, E." Caelan called from the driver's side.

Didn't have to ask him twice. He jumped in the car, slamming the door shut behind him. The lot was quiet. There weren't even that many cars, surprisingly. Except the one that conveniently pulled in catty-corner at their front bumper, blocking them in.

Eli's hand went to the gun at his back, Caelan's groped under the seat.

A man jumped out of the driver's door and ran around to the other side, threw open the door and gingerly extracted a little girl whose sobs Eli could hear in the SUV. The man held up a finger to them signaling to give him a minute.

"Son of a bitch," Caelan hissed and jerked his thumb over his shoulder. Another car had driven up, blocking them from behind. What the fuck was going on? They went from no cars to a lot full.

"Can you believe this?" Pissed at the turn of events, he searched their surroundings.

Nikki kept her eyes closed when she really wanted to watch Eli and Caelan. Whatever they were talking about was sure putting Eli in a grouchy mood.

"Are you all right?" Eli asked.

Nikki opened her eyes. Had she made a noise? The concern in his voice was genuine. She searched his face. His eyes seemed to glow a golden brown. She knew they turned even more gold when he was angry. How would they look when aroused?

"Hello?" He waved his hand.

Crap.

"I'm fine." Jesus, had she sounded husky there? She cleared her throat. "I won't break, E."

"I'll break you in all right," he muttered.

Nikki shook her head, trying to reduce the drug-induced cobwebs. He hadn't just said that, had he?

"What did—"

"You heard me. Now settle in, it's a long trip."

"Geez, E, I don't live in Timbuktu," she muttered, choosing to ignore his outrageous comment for the moment.

He and Caelan mumbled something she didn't understand. Werewolf-ese? She giggled, earning an eyeful from both men, each sporting a cocked eyebrow. If only they knew the direction of her thoughts.

"Why don't you go to sleep, Nikki-Raine."

She jerked upright in her seat. "You don't have to get all growly," she said, sobering. What the hell had crawled up his shorts? His fur must be getting itchy. She laughed again, unable to hold it in. God, just the image of him covered in fur was ridiculous. Derek had to be mistaken. Turning into an animal wasn't possible.

This time Eli's lip curled in the corner revealing too sharp teeth, while his eyes seemed to glow and his entire body shook with a low rumble. Nikki's eyes widened. One minute he was all over her, practically sucking her lips off, the next he was madder than hell. What was up with that? She hadn't asked him to take on this responsibility. He was the one who bullied his way in, made her reveal herself to him when she didn't want to.

So fuck him. If he didn't like it, he could get the hell out.

Her eyes burned in mortification, and her chest hurt. Not that she'd ever let him see how much he affected her. Bastard. Nikki slumped down in the seat and turned to stare out into the sunny day.

The back window shattered behind her. She screamed in reaction. Her cheek tingled and she raised both hands to her face, yelping again when a tearing pain seared across her wounded shoulder. The blood drained from her head. Through the thick fog enveloping her brain, it sounded like Eli and Caelan were shouting.

Christ had one of them been shot? "Eli?" she tried to yell but wasn't sure if the words actually came out.

A loud squeal pierced her ears and her head was thrown into the window, then she felt nothing.

Chapter Six

Eli hurdled the console into the backseat. Fuck. Nikki was too quiet. Not even out of the parking lot yet and the asshole had stolen advantage. If he hadn't fucking kissed her. If he had just shoved her pretty little ass in the car and taken off like they were supposed to.

Son of a *bitch.*

"Is she hit?" Caelan demanded.

Eli couldn't see straight. Nikki was so still, slumped over, her head leaning toward the floor. He'd killed her. Sure as shit as if he'd shot her himself. His heart pounded, sweat coated his forehead, his hands shook.

"Is she fucking hit, E?"

Eli couldn't answer. Not through the tightness constricting his throat. Caelan took a corner, throwing Eli over Nikki's body and into the window.

Shit. Pain sliced through his chin.

Nikki moaned.

Alive. She was alive.

"Eli!" Caelan shouted.

"I don't know," Eli yelled back. He turned Nikki onto her back, careful not to fling her head around any more than Caelan was doing swerving the SUV back and forth through traffic.

Her eyes fluttered for a second before closing all the way and a puff of air separated her sweet lips. Lips he'd cradled with his own minutes earlier. An angry red scratch slashed across one cheek. Not deep, probably glass. Didn't look like a bullet wound.

He'd kill the motherfucker for drawing blood on his mate a second time.

The same way he'd kill the three assholes who'd attacked her. Eight months wasn't too long for the trail to go cold. He'd bet money if they'd tried once, they'd tried it again with some other unlucky female.

"God damn it, Eli, if you don't—"

"Not shot. A scratch on her cheek. That's it."

"Then why in the shit is she so quiet?"

"She fainted." *I think.*

Caelan slammed his fist on the steering wheel. "You'd think one of us could actually mate with a female who's not in the sights of a whacko."

"You'd think," Eli murmured, caressing his thumb along the scratch. Nikki sighed and unconsciously turned her face into his hand. At least in sleep she felt comfortable with him. He'd have to work on her during her waking hours because whether she liked him or not, he was going to stick to her like glue.

Eli clenched his jaw and looked up. Something in the door caught his attention and he leaned forward. A cut in the leather. He fingered it apart. Dull metal gleamed back at him. The bullet.

He'd come so close to losing her. Another couple of inches and that bullet would have been lodged in her brain instead of the door panel. He punched the back of the seat, throwing Caelan forward.

"There's a bullet lodged in your door." His teeth hurt from the pressure he exerted on them.

"Better than the back of her head," Caelan growled. "What the fuck happened?" he shouted into his cell phone.

Eli hadn't even noticed him making a call.

"Do more than check out the angle the shot came from. Find the shooter. I thought everything had been cleared. My brother almost lost his mate by getting her fucking head blown off."

Eli idly stroked Nikki's black cap of hair, loving the smooth silkiness of it between his fingers, and held her hand. He inhaled her scent again, not that it had ever left his brain. When he finally got her beneath him and marked her with his teeth, she'd never be able to hide from him. Her essence would be that strong within him. Put her in a stadium filled with forty thousand people and he'd be able to follow his nose to her seat.

His cock hardened. Not now. Not when she lay here unconscious after someone had taken another potshot at her.

"I'll say fuck as many times as I fucking want to. Do you even understand the implications of what just happened?"

Eli smiled. His twin was not a Prime you wanted to go up against and since many of the people at the hospital were shifters, heads were undoubtedly going to roll.

"She's part of our pack now, she's Eli's mate even if he hasn't announced it yet."

Eli stiffened. Damn. There's something he hadn't thought about. He wanted time to have her to himself. Meeting the pack as his other half could wait.

"Fine. Make sure it gets leaked that their witness is dead. She's gone. Tell the detective assigned to her case to shout it to the press. Maybe this is the only way to keep her alive. Let the bastard think he won." Caelan stared back at Eli through the mirror. His brother had to have seen the way Eli's face drained of blood, leaving him pale and lightheaded at the mention of telling everyone Nikki had died.

He swallowed and shook his head. Caelan clicked the phone shut.

"It was the only thing I could think of, E."

"No, no it's good." He tightened his hold on Nikki's fingers. Nodding once, he said, "It needed to be done." Eli clambered back into the front seat with a great amount of reluctance. "Looks like she's down for the count."

"Helps that we slipped her that sleeping pill before we left."

"She needs the sleep. Her eyes look haunted. I bet she hasn't slept since it happened." He twisted to pull his seat belt on. "Plus, this way, I don't have to explain to her why we're headed to the ranch."

Caelan laughed. "Nikki's gonna kick your ass."

"She'll get over it." Eli turned and watched her sleep. Peaceful at last, other than the red line across her cheek. And the bullet wound. And the obvious concern she had with him learning what had happened to her.

Not so insurmountable. In the next few lifetimes. He probably would never get over her being attacked, having some other man's hands on her perfect little body.

Eli clenched his fists.

"I'll make sure she gets over it."

CB80

Nikki's eyes flew open. A steady rock and hum combined with the low ramblings of some country music station and the constant sensation of an open window flooded her senses. She squinted at the bright sunlight filtering through the glass beside her just like the memories were doing in her brain.

Someone had shot at her. Again. When would this end?

And where the hell were they? She shifted in her seat and looked around. The rear window had a hole with spider web cracks radiating off it where the bullet had entered the SUV. Her entire body shook. Way too close for comfort. Nothing outside the car seemed familiar. Two-lane highway, lots of open land, space for miles. Not like the businesses that crowded Highway 70 until her exit for home. Even then houses lined the road here and there.

How long had she been out? Her cheek burned when she swiped a hand over her face. For a moment, her heart pounded. With her fingertips, Nikki traced a fine, raised line across her left cheek.

Great. Just what she needed, another scar. Maybe they'd cancel each other out. Her fingers came away clean so it must only be a scratch. The fear dissipated, leaving behind a tremble in her hands.

Wiping her sweaty palm along her thigh, Nikki sighed and closed her eyes. Why did her brain feel like mush? Like the time she'd had too much to drink, or when she'd taken that painkiller...

"You drugged me."

Eli whipped around, his mouth opening and closing like a fish. "Hey, Nikki-Raine—"

"Don't you Nikki-Raine me, Eli."

"I didn't, I mean, Caelan did it," he sputtered. Damn but it felt good to put him in his place. Eli pointed to his brother, a sheepish look on his face.

"Some man you are." Nikki focused on the back of the driver's seat and tried to get more comfortable. "You sound like a girl, you big baby."

Caelan snorted a laugh. When Nikki looked back up, Eli's eyes were narrowed.

"Don't think I won't be showing you just how much of a man I am, Nikki," he said softly.

She dropped her gaze. Her belly quivered, and her nipples tightened to hard points beneath her T-shirt. Braless because of her shoulder, the tips brushed erotically against the cotton. Damn the man for making her feel like this now, in the midst of all this chaos. Especially now when she'd convinced herself he'd never like her after all the things that had happened to her. He was proving her wrong at every turn with his flat-out suggestions, glances, touches. And the kisses. Melt-her-into-the-ground, I'm-going-to-eat-you-up kisses. Who knew the man could kiss like that?

And suddenly she was jealous of all the other women who might know exactly how he could kiss.

"Look at me, Nikki-Raine."

Her cheeks reddened. How could she? Thank God he wasn't a mind reader. She crossed her arms over her chest so he couldn't see the state of her breast's arousal. Nikki had to stop thinking about him this way, lusting after him like a lovesick puppy. Sympathy. That's what all this was about. He felt bad for her and the situation and was trying anything possible to get her mind off it. Right? What other reason would he have for acting this way after all the years they'd known each other?

"Nikki. Raine." The sensual, steely command in his voice compelled her to look at him.

His eyes seemed to glow beneath the incredible eyelashes she'd always envied. Eli was, quite possibly, the most yummy man alive. More so even than his twin whom she'd only met a few times. There was something extra about Eli that made her want him in the most elemental way. No man had ever been able to fill the void like she knew he could. In the past, sex had simply been a way to distract her attention from the man more apt to give her a noogie than a mind-blowing orgasm.

Nikki's clit tingled to the point she had to clench her thighs together. She silently damned him again. Lifting her chin, she hissed, "What?"

The bastard smiled. She itched to slap it off his face. He wasn't allowed to be happy in light of her emotional turmoil.

"You and I will talk later."

"What, you afraid big brother might hear you?" Caelan asked.

"Big brother, my ass," Eli muttered, turning his gaze on Caelan.

Caelan laughed. "As your Prime—"

"Shut the fuck up."

"What'd I say?"

"I'm not ready to tell her yet," Eli ground out beneath his breath. "It's not like this is the best of places to talk about it."

Nikki looked from one brother to the other. She felt like she was watching tennis.

"Well, you've got to tell her sometime, and you probably shouldn't do it the way I told Tieran. It got kind of messy."

"Yeah, fucking your mate for the first time on the countertop can get that way. I think I can handle it, thanks."

"Boys!"

Silence, finally. Arguing over...what exactly? She had no clue. They may as well have been speaking German for all she could understand.

"Do you guys hear yourselves? Bickering like five-year-olds. Caelan"—Nikki eyed him in the rearview mirror—"what the hell is a Prime? And, Eli, if you've got something to tell me, spit it out. Don't go all pansy-assed on me."

Neither one spoke and silence reigned yet again. At least both of them had the decency to look contrite. She sighed, knowing from past experiences that Eli wouldn't talk until he was damn good and ready. Hardheaded...beast.

"Where are we?" Changing the subject seemed a good thing to do. "Nothing looks familiar."

"We're going home," he growled.

Good to know his surly attitude had dissipated. "Hey, if you don't want me around, by all means, drop me off." *Please God, don't drop me off.*

Eli jerked around. "I'm not even going to dignify that with a response," he snarled.

Her heart thumped at his behavior before settling back into a more normal rhythm. She wouldn't let him scare her. Even if the tone did remind her of... *Christ, don't go there, Nikki.* Eli was nothing like those men.

Swallowing, Nikki tried for a nonchalant approach. "You certainly don't sound like you want me around," she muttered.

Great. Now who sounds like a five-year-old? Why don't you sniffle while you're at it?

"You're pushin' it, Nikki-Raine. Don't make me come back there and spank your ass, 'cause I'll do it, bullet wound or not."

Her breath lodged in her throat and she had to close her eyes. Imagining his hands anywhere on her body made the folds between her legs slick. If only he'd said shit like this sooner. They could have gotten together before he left on his trip. At least then she'd know where she stood right now. Not that he wasn't making it abundantly clear where he'd like them to be.

"Do you have any idea what kind of mess you're in, baby?"

Oh, God, please don't call me that.

Besides, she knew exactly the kind of shit she was in. She'd seen her friends, seen the carnage and waste of life. The image would forever be burned in her mind. Nikki doubted anything would ever make it go away. Just as nothing had made the incident from eight months ago go away. If anybody wanted to catch this sick bastard, it was her for not being able to do anything to help her friends.

"He's shot at you twice now, Nikki, I won't underestimate him again. If I have to lock you in our bedroom until he's caught to keep you safe, I will."

A bed sounded wonderful. Her boxers, a tank top, nice soft sheets. She'd sleep for a week. If she ever got to sleep again, anyway. Damn. Nikki ground her palms over her eyes, fighting back the tears threatening to take over.

A strange mewling sound filled the car. She realized a second later she'd made the sound. Safe. That's all she really wanted. To feel safe for the first time in all these months. Nikki had a hunch only one man could do that for her. Eli. She reached for the scratch on her cheek again. He was right. If anyone could protect her, he could. Her lips still tingled from his earlier kiss. The kiss that had left her lips swollen and wanting more. A kiss that hadn't been a dream. The one that made her belly flip-flop like no other man had ever done.

Wait a minute. Suddenly she was thrust back into reality. Had he said...?

"What do you mean, *our* room?" She winced at the huskiness in her voice.

Eli shifted around again so she stared at the back of his head.

"I'm done staying away from you, Nikki-Raine. You're mine." This time he growled. Growled. That's the only way she could describe it.

Her heart returned to pounding. At this rate she'd have a heart attack and die before they even made it home. She shook her head. His house, not home, his house.

An ache grew in her clit, stretching through her abdomen and licking down her legs. She couldn't have been more shocked by his possessive declaration than if he had shouted, "I'm going to fuck you all night long when we get there."

Nikki fought the urge to cover her ears from her own thoughts.

"Where are we going?" she asked again. She'd never been to his house before, not in all the years Derek and he had been friends. Nikki had always just believed it was due to his private nature.

"I told you, home."

"Which is where, exactly?" she said between her teeth. Damn stubborn, mule-headed...pig. If he wanted to be sharp with her, she'd return the favor. She certainly hadn't asked to be here.

"The ranch. We're almost there."

Yeah, that helped.

Her scent was driving him insane. Eli had to get out of the car before he did something stupid. Like jump in the back and sink his rock-hard cock into what he knew would be her hot, wet pussy. Either that or he'd shift right in front her. That would go over well. One minute a man, the next an animal. Talk about fainting.

Eli gritted his lengthening teeth and willed them back to human. He would not show her this in the confines of the car. He smiled. Or show up in her bed as a wolf after their first mating. Not like Caelan had done with his mate.

It didn't help that she was being so damn feisty and argumentative. He loved sparring with her, always had, but he would not give in when it came to her life.

As a shifter, protecting his mate was his duty, an honor, and so far he'd done a piss-poor job of it.

Fuck.

He should have done more, hired someone to watch her while he was gone.

"Eli, I don't want to put your family in any danger."

Caelan snorted next to him.

"Take me to a hotel."

Like hell. Put his mate in some no-good hotel? Never. "You do remember that Caelan and I own a security business, right?" he asked, mocking her. She knew damn well what he did for a living.

"Don't patronize me, Eli. I'm talking about your parents, and isn't Caelan's wife expecting a baby soon? I thought they lived with you."

"Cael and Tieran live there, yes, but Mom and Dad have their own place."

"Trust me, Nikki," Caelan added, "I will never let anything happen to my ma...wife."

Eli glanced at his brother. Asshole had almost let the cat out of the bag. Again. Eli wasn't ready for that discussion yet.

"You'll be safer at the ranch where I can keep a better eye on you," he muttered, still looking at his brother. He turned to her. Her face was a mixture of glaring daggers, fear and hunger. Hunger for him. Her nipples were hard and the succulent scent of her arousal permeated the car. Good thing Caelan was immune to anything but his own mate, or they'd both be panting right now. Every minute that went by made Eli more and more possessive of Nikki.

They stared at each other for long, heated seconds. Over the whistling of wind from the hole in the back window, he heard Nikki's heart pounding. He saw the blood coursing through the vein along the smooth skin of her long, slender throat. She licked her lips, her gaze dropping to his mouth. Damn but she made it really hard to stay in the front seat and keep his hands off her.

The SUV slowed to make a sharp turn, bumping over the irregular gravel road that led to their home. The land called to him, as it always did, urging him to shift and run. Now more than ever since he'd been gone for so long.

Eli broke the connection between him and Nikki and faced the front, looking around to see any changes he might have missed. Everything looked pretty much the same, with the exception of some new fencing along the pasture to his right. A few horses dotted the land, lazily chewing and mulling about.

God, but he had missed this place. He wasn't ever taking on another assignment like the one he'd just left. Of course, he wouldn't have to now that he had a mate. Nikki would come first and foremost from now on. And if he'd acknowledged her eight months ago, maybe none of this would have happened. He'd have been here to protect her. Or at the very least, help her get through the tragedy.

"How far away is it?" Nikki's soft but urgent voice broke through his musings.

"Not far."

"Okay, 'cause I gotta go."

Eli barked out in laughter. There was the little spitfire he knew and loved.

"Stupid men," she muttered, drawing out another round of laughter from both he and Caelan.

"I fail to see what's funny."

"Nothing, sweetheart."

She scowled at him. "I'm not your sweetheart."

Her words sobered him. "You will always be my sweetheart." He couldn't prevent the glow he knew took over his eyes and heard the gasp she made when it happened. Her eyes widened and she shrank back in her seat. Then her lids narrowed as if inspecting him, trying to decide if what she saw was real or not.

The SUV rocked through another series of potholes and Nikki grimaced as her shoulder bounced against the door.

"Jesus, Caelan, fix the road, why don't you?" It killed him to see Nikki hurting, especially because of something as simple as the road.

"Oh, right, it's my fault there's bumps in the same road you've bumped over since the day you were born," Caelan snarled.

"Then let's get the damn thing paved," Eli growled back. "It's not like we can't afford it!"

"Did you forget *why* it's not paved?" Caelan hissed.

"Yoohoo, boys. Hello, five-year-olds again. Get over it, Eli, I'm fine."

Eli's breath practically heaved from his chest. He needed to run. Confined for hours of plane rides and then being on the go since landing hadn't done him a bit of good. There was a reason they didn't pave their roads, a selfish one, but hey. They didn't like the way the pavement felt beneath their paws. Everyone in his pack preferred natural to manmade so, aside from the fences to keep their horses from scattering, most of the land was kept as wild as possible.

"Oh my God, is that your house? It's huge."

"I told you it wouldn't be a problem," Eli agreed.

"It's beautiful."

Despite the ugliness of what had brought her to his home, he heard the sincerity in her voice and his pride lifted. Caelan brought the SUV to a stop on the gravel drive and the three of them sat, seemingly suspended in time. Eli was the first to break the strange moment.

"All right then. Let's get out of the car, shall we?" He went around the hood, jumping out of the way to avoid the driver's door his brother threw open.

Nikki still sat, looking out the front window at the house, when he opened the door to help her out. He bent in to see what she saw.

"It's a house, Nikki-Raine," he whispered, tickling her ear with his lips. She smelled so good. It was all he could do to keep from burying his head in the crook of her shoulder and laying her across the seat to have his way with her.

She squirmed to dislodge his mouth from her earlobe. "It's big."

Eli shrugged. "Yeah, well, we planned on having lots of runts running around one day."

Her gaze flew to his. "Runts? We? You're both going to...stay here? Together? With families?"

"Breathe." He wrapped his hand around the back of her neck, soothing her with his thumb along her rapid pulse point.

"I'm just shocked I guess."

"Why? You live with your brother, why does it shock you that I choose to live with mine?"

"I wouldn't live with my brother if I didn't have to, and you are talking about raising your families together, not sharing an apartment."

Eli sighed and dropped his chin to his chest, thinking about the best way to broach the subject. How easy it would be to just come out and say, *That's the way a pack works. We like to be close to our families, to keep our young within reach and share in the responsibilities of raising the offspring that would one day be an active part of a shifter community.*

Damn it sounded so good in his head. Reality wouldn't quite work out the same way. At least he'd give her something tangible to be truly shocked about.

Lifting his face to hers again, he changed the subject. "Over there," he said pointing to the right side, "is our wing, and that side is Caelan and Tieran's. There's a kitchen, living room, dining room and den along the back, but each wing has its own private area for eating or whatever, if you don't feel like socializing. We made it that way so we still have our privacy when we need it."

Chapter Seven

Our wing? Nikki swallowed. With every word she was getting closer and closer to believing he wanted a relationship with her despite everything that had happened. Not just every word. Every kiss, every look. Simply put, she believed the man wanted her. And she more than wanted him.

The front door flew open and an obviously way pregnant woman waddled out. Nikki's stomach churned. This was not a good idea. No matter what Caelan said, she was putting his family in danger. She stared at the pretty woman who rubbed idly at the small of her back. Caelan's wife. Had to be.

To her right, a horse whinnied softly, the sound carrying on the breeze. The mixed scents of horse, hay, leather and pine wafted across her nose. Nikki closed her eyes and sucked in a deep breath. She was home.

Her eyes flew open. Where in the hell had that come from? A bird called from far away, a testimony to the peaceful silence surrounding her. Eli's hard chest pressed against her back and she sagged into him.

"I know you can feel it, Nikki-Raine. Let it all go and relax. Nothing can hurt you here," Eli whispered against her ear. The words sent a shiver down her spine.

He was right. Nothing could hurt her here on this land. It would help rid her of her determination to hide from the world because it had gone to shit on her.

His arm wrapped around her midsection, adding strength and keeping her from sloughing to the floor. How she'd slept most of the way here and now felt tired enough to sleep for days, she didn't know. She wanted a pillow and a warm blanket and she'd be good to go.

"You're wilting, sweetheart. Let's get you inside."

Unable to speak, she nodded. Eli bent behind her and scooped her into his arms. She squeaked in protest but a second later sank into his unyielding hold and laid her hand above his heart. Incredibly she felt his heartbeat stutter.

"You're mine," he growled not for the first time and she wondered about it.

For years Nikki had loved him from afar. She'd been getting close to telling him how she really felt when he'd had to leave on his trip, and she hadn't gotten the chance. Then she'd been attacked, and it had seemed at the time she had no option but to let him go. Not so anymore. He didn't care about her face being scarred so why should she?

If being with him now meant losing her heart to him later when he moved on to someone else, she'd take whatever she could get.

Nikki knew Eli. Knew how many beautiful women flitted in and out of his life. Her hand fisted in his shirt. She didn't want to know the details of those hags. Eli was hers now and she'd keep him for as long as he let her.

And then she would slowly die on the inside when he decided he'd had enough.

"I won't leave you, Nikki-Raine."

She startled in his arms, making him stagger a step. "How did you—"

He snorted. "Honey, I can read you like an open book. You leave it all out there in the open for everyone to see. Always have. That's why I'm wondering how you made it eight months without telling anybody all the details about what happened. Me, especially, which, by the way, I'm supremely pissed about."

Nikki swallowed as Eli took the steps up to the porch. She didn't want to have this conversation. She wanted to snuggle deeper into his arms and forget about everything else.

Tears welled up, threatening to spill. Not in a million years would she be able to forget.

"I know you told them the basics, but you've never talked about what you felt, have you? Told them the raw terror you've had all this time. They've seen it in you, but you've kept the words bottled up inside, haven't you? No more secrets, Nikki."

She started to speak but was interrupted by the woman who'd come out to meet them.

"Eli, good to see you again."

Eli bent at the waist, giving a small bow, and Nikki clung to his shoulders to keep from falling on her ass.

"Tieran. Damn that's a big baby."

Tieran gasped and slapped at his shoulder.

Moron. "Jesus, Eli, can you be a bigger idiot?" Nikki wiggled out of his hold, planting her feet on the ground and shrugging Eli off. He relented only slightly, keeping one arm wrapped around her middle in an almost protective hold. She cleared her throat and lifted her good arm.

"I'm Nikki."

"Tieran."

Eyeing each other up, they shook hands. Tieran didn't look like the type of woman to cause trouble, but...

"Did you really think Eli had killed all those girls?"

Foot in mouth. Had to be the drugs talking. Eli's arm squeezed her belly, jarring her arm and therefore her shoulder, making her groan. Tieran's face turned all shades of red before she lifted her chin and pulled Nikki's hand into the crook of her elbow.

Tieran gasped and something in her eyes sparkled when she looked at Eli. A second later she went into a trance. That's the only word to describe what happened. Her eyes glazed over and she stiffened up. Tieran's fingers crushed Nikki's hand in a painful grip.

"Oh, Christ. Now look what you've done," Eli murmured.

"What? What did I do?"

Tieran let out a gush of air and focused on Nikki. Her face was pale where it had been flushed a minute ago, and her whole body positively vibrated.

Tieran swallowed audibly. "It was dark and small. An enclosed area." She looked to Eli, a question in her eyes.

Eli simply nodded once, his jaw jumping with the force he was putting on it.

"What's she talking—"

"My own. What are you doing out here?" Caelan asked in a tender tone, cutting Nikki off.

"Stuff it," Tieran groaned. All traces of her weirding out were, poof, gone. "While you were out playing chauffeur, I've been sitting in this house suffocating. Now you're back and I'm outside." Tieran smiled sweetly at her husband and Nikki had to laugh. It appeared Caelan was just as big an oaf as Eli. Should have known it, coming from identical twins.

"What happened to the back of the car, Caelan?" Tieran asked, trying to tug Nikki out of Eli's grasp.

He wasn't having any part of letting her go.

"Oh. Nikki was shot at at the hospital. We narrowly escaped with her life, and here we are."

Tieran gasped. Her jaw dropped open and she pinned him with the evil eye. "So not funny."

Eli sighed. "No, not funny, but true." He stepped forward, forcing the three of them into the doorway since they were all still connected.

How Eli thought all of them were going to fit was beyond her. A dance ensued. In a bizarre *The Three Stooges* way, they shimmied through the doorway until, like a cork popping out of a champagne bottle, they came unstuck and spilled into the foyer.

Tieran kept hold of Nikki's arm. Eli had to let go or fall on them. He latched onto the doorframe to keep from stumbling, only to get bumped from behind by his brother.

"Damn, Tieran, I don't know what it is with you and doors, but don't be bringing that shit into this house," Caelan grumbled.

She did let go of Nikki this time, to swat at her husband.

"I didn't do it, he did."

Living here was going to be like living in a kindergarten classroom. Nikki hung her head, weariness doing its best to take over. And she still wanted to know what Tieran had meant about a dark closet. No, not a closet. She'd said enclosed space. Why had she suddenly blurted that out anyway?

Caelan grabbed the back of his wife's neck and hauled her closer, attracting Nikki's attention. He proceeded to kiss his wife senseless. Nikki's entire being thrummed just watching the two of them. Feeling like a voyeur, she turned away. Eli's formidable body got in the way.

Before she knew what was happening, Eli crushed his mouth to hers. She melted into him. His arms surrounded her, pinning her to him. One hand wandered lower and lower until he cupped her bottom and urged her closer still.

His lips cajoled, his tongue plundered, taking what it wanted and accepting nothing less. She opened to him and allowed it to happen. In fact, couldn't stop it from happening. Nikki gave as good as she got. Her tongue slid over his, learning his mouth. He had the sharpest teeth...

The thick length of his cock pressed into her belly and made her wonder how it would feel against her skin. Or better yet, in her mouth.

Eli devoured her, making her lose all semblance of reality. Only when a shooting pain seized her shoulder did she break apart, yelping.

"Shit. I'm sorry." He grabbed for her and hugged her gently to him, kissing the top of her head. By the time she'd caught her breath and looked back up, Caelan and Tieran had disappeared, leaving them standing alone inside the still open front door.

Her knees shook. Not from the pain, but from sheer exhaustion. If she didn't get to a bed soon, she'd end up on the floor.

"Uh-uh. Not on my watch." Eli read her mind again and scooped her back into his arms.

She sagged in his hold. If he wanted to carry around her dead weight, who was she to stop him?

"How come you've never brought me here?" she asked, yawning.

She walked her fingers over one of his pecs, giggling when his nipple beaded beneath the taut fabric of his shirt. Nikki traced it with her fingernail and laughed when Eli stumbled with a grunt. His arms tightened around her, squeezing the breath from her lungs.

"Squished here."

"Tempted here."

"Tempted?" Nikki lifted her head to better see his face.

His eyebrows slanted together as if he were in pain.

"Yes, you little minx. Don't even pretend to not know what you do to me." His footsteps slowed when they reached a closed door, and he propped her against the wall to turn the knob. He pushed the door in with his toe and after they'd entered, kicked it closed with his heel.

She batted her eyelashes, ready to play with him. "Why, Eli, whatever are you talking about?"

His chest vibrated along her rib cage.

"If you weren't hurt, I'd have you naked and spread out on our bed in about two point three seconds."

Nikki's breath caught. Her pussy flooded in want. Need. She needed him like a drowning man needed air.

Part of her felt like if she didn't have him soon, she'd die.

She was addled. It had to be the drugs. Yes, for the last couple of years she'd ogled him behind his back, yearned to be with him, but lately her body, and her heart, had been craving him.

Eli slowly lowered her to the biggest bed she'd ever seen. The worn, frayed quilt looked as though it had been stitched by hand a century ago. She ran a hand over the multicolored pattern, feeling its softness. It obviously wasn't made for the bed since it barely came to the edge.

"This must mean something to you."

He shrugged. "My great-grandmother made it a long time ago. It's comfy."

She had to laugh. "What a manly thing to say, E." Nikki glanced at him. For a second he stared back, his nostrils flaring.

"When you're ready for manly, I'll show you manly." He traced a path down her cheek and cupped her chin with a rough palm. "Damn you're beautiful."

Nikki cocked her head. "What makes you say these things now?"

"What do you mean?"

"We've known each other for years, E. You never talked to me before the way you are now."

His thumb grazed her jawline, giving her shivers. "I say them now because I wasn't ready to say them before."

"Why?"

"There are things you don't know about me, Nikki. Things I tell very few people that you might not understand." His thumb tracked to her ear and flicked lightly at the lobe.

Her stomach fluttered in uneasiness. Could what Derek said at the hospital be true? Was Eli really a...werewolf? Was it even possible?

She had to know. "Are you a—"

"Shhh." Eli silenced her with a long finger across her lips. His eyes glittered with desire, making her clit tingle in even more awareness. "I'll answer all your questions, sweetheart. Later. You need to sleep right now."

Her brain scrambled, turning foggy as if he'd put a spell on her. That was about as likely as him turning into a big dog. "But I—"

He shook his head. "Later."

Eli stood before her, close enough she could smell him. She loved the way he smelled. Had stolen one of his shirts a few years back so she could smell him whenever she wanted to. He was all male. Made her want to sink to her knees in front of him. That would shock the hell out of him for sure.

Nikki smiled. What would he say? What would he do? Push her away? Unzip?

Probably laugh his ass off.

No. On second thought, he wouldn't. He'd unzip and cradle her head in his hands and guide her mouth to him.

God, she had to stop thinking like this.

He smoothed his hands down her arms, raising the hairs on her skin and leaving a tingle everywhere his fingers touched. She sat there like a bump on a log, her heart pounding, stomach twirling. If only he'd touch her breasts. Just once. Surely that would put out the fire burning at her nipples. Without looking, she knew the hardened tips were protruding through her shirt.

He'd have to be a complete idiot not to see it. When she looked into his eyes, she knew he wasn't an idiot. His gaze was riveted on said nipples and his jaw ticked. One finger wandered from its spot on her upper arm and slowly traversed her chest, following the contours of her breast to circle the nipple there. His Adam's apple bobbed in his throat.

A moan filled the silence. Nikki closed her eyes on the exquisite feeling of his touch and dropped her head back.

The caress disappeared, leaving her feeling empty somehow. A second later, Eli tugged at the hem of her shirt.

Her moment of insanity fled and she jerked upright. "What...what are you doing?"

He smiled. "Helping you get your shirt off over your shoulder."

"Oh." Oh. The cad didn't seem at all affected by their little interlude. Of course he was helping. That's what friends do. They help.

But friends don't play with a friend's nipples, she chided herself. Enough with the "woe is me". *If the man didn't want you, he wouldn't be here now and his eyes wouldn't be glowing with desire.* He wanted her, plain and simple. She didn't think there'd be any more hiding from Eli Graham.

Somehow with his help, which involved more touches than were actually needed, they managed to get her shirt off with minimal duress.

"Beautiful," he said again.

Had her back arched? Suddenly self-conscious, Nikki covered herself with her arms.

"Uh-uh. Do not cover yourself with me. Mine." He lifted her arms away and held them without hurting her.

Why, oh why, did her pussy clench whenever he said that word? There was something raw and possessive in his eyes as he devoured every bare inch of her skin with his gaze. Her cheeks flushed under his intense perusal.

Eli dropped to his knees. Nikki jumped with the action. The position put him at eye level with her breasts. Her nipples betrayed her by puckering into even tighter points.

As if in slow motion, he lowered his head to her chest, stopping a mere inch from the almost painfully full tip. His lip curled back to reveal long white teeth. Teeth that seemed longer and sharper than any she'd ever seen. Her breath snagged in her throat and she shook her head. It couldn't be.

Oblivious to her thoughts, Eli zeroed in on his target and wrapped his lips around one areola. Nikki hummed in satisfaction.

Yes. Yes, yes, yes. A thousand times yes.

His tongue rasped over the sensitive nipple and her toes curled. Again and again he sucked at her, drawing her deep into his mouth. Nikki twisted her arms in his hands, trying to draw away from him, and when she finally succeeded, she slapped at his shoulders in time to his rhythmic pulls. Her heels dug into the bedframe.

Eli spread her knees further with little effort and settled more comfortably between her thighs like he belonged there. And he did, no question.

She wanted more.

He moved to the other breast, lavishing it with the same attention as the first. Nikki jabbed her fingers into his thickly muscled upper arms and held on. Each tug to her breast replicated itself in her pussy. Even she could smell herself.

With a flick of his wrist, Eli undid the tie of her pants and slid his hand inside. His fingers tangled in the curls shielding her pussy before finding and laying claim to the tight bundle of nerves at the top.

Nikki tilted her hips, leaning back and hissing at the twinge in her shoulder when she propped herself up with it. She shook it off. The position gave him better access and no way would she impede his magic. Never before had a man made her feel this way. Every inch of her body sang praises to the god with his hand down her pants.

Eli's hand slid lower, cupping her mound and gliding through her slippery folds. And still he kept up the powerful suction at her breast. The twin sensations threatened to shatter her. A long finger penetrated her while his palm rubbed her clit.

Just a little more and she'd come. She groaned and grunted with each pass that brought her nearer. Almost...there. Almost...

Throwing her head back, Nikki gasped at the sudden sharp pain at the top of her breast and screamed with her simultaneous orgasm. Eli pumped his finger in and out, carrying her over the crest and beyond until her heartbeat settled.

"Oh, my God," she breathed. What had just happened?

A warm tongue licked at her breast, soothing where she'd felt the pinch of his teeth. He'd bitten her.

If him biting her had led her to that colossal pinnacle of release, he could bite her anytime he wanted to.

Unable to sit any longer, Nikki collapsed onto her back and stared at the ceiling. The action pulled Eli's finger from her drenched pussy, firing off sensations throughout her slit. She bucked upward, ignoring the pulling at her shoulder, and bit her lip.

When she finally got her breathing under control, Nikki tilted her chin and gazed at Eli, still kneeling between her thighs. He looked like a damned Cheshire cat who'd gotten the cream.

He had. And while she watched, he slowly lifted his fingers to his mouth and licked them clean.

Chapter Eight

"In local news, there was a shooting at St. Mary's hospital at four o'clock this afternoon. A gunshot was fired from a fourth floor window in a part of the hospital currently under reconstruction. The victim, an unidentified, adult female, was shot through the head and killed. Police tell us tonight that the woman was a witness in a recent murder investigation. They cite this as probable cause for the shooting. The woman was being escorted at the time by two bodyguards who drove off when the shooting started, but were unable to save the woman's life. She died en route to another hospital. Police aren't releasing any further information, pending further investigation."

He hit the mute button and slid the remote across the polished surface of the coffee table. Smiling, he picked up his tumbler and sank back into the buttery soft leather of his couch.

Luck had been with him after all.

He swirled the amber-colored whiskey, sniffing in appreciation, before taking a swig. The liquor burned a sweet path to his stomach. Closing his eyes, he inhaled.

"Here's to a job well done." He saluted the air and propped his feet on the table.

He'd been on edge the entire afternoon, waiting for the news. This news. The fucking cops had been tightlipped at the hospital earlier, and speculation had run rampant about what had happened. Immediately following the incident, in fact, he hadn't even made it back to the ER, they'd been shoved into lockdown. No one in or out.

Everyone had been questioned, including him.

"No, officer, I didn't see anything." He chuckled. They weren't ever going to figure anything out. Not about him.

But hey, he'd made the news tonight at least. Not all of his murders were picked up. Sometimes there were just too many other things happening and he got skipped.

He gripped the crystal in his fist, squeezing hard enough he thought the glass might shatter. Easing his hold, he lowered the drink to his knee.

It stung, those times when he didn't make the news. Made him feel like he wasn't doing a good enough job.

Idly, he traced the rim of the glass with his thumb and sucked in his bottom lip. His mother had never thought he was good enough.

With a gut-wrenching yell, he threw the delicate crystal across the room. It shattered with a satisfying crash against the wall, each piece tinkling to the hardwood floor. The whiskey sluiced down the pale wallpaper, discoloring it.

The bitch. Once again, his mother had won. Made him think about her and their shitheap of a life. Made him destroy something that was beautiful. Why did she make him do it? Why did she still have a fucking hold on him after all these years?

He rubbed his eyes until they ached and his breathing slowed, and forced himself to remember the fitting way he'd released himself from her physically demoralizing clutches. She would never again grind him under the heel of her whore shoes.

Sitting upright, he stared at the scattering of Polaroid's on the table. Each one as precious to him as the next. Each one a reminder of how powerful he really was. He fingered them, spreading them out and visualizing each woman in his mind. Whores, all of them. He figured a woman was only good for one thing—sex. They sure as shit hadn't been put on Earth for their brains. Just like his mother, they were more a bane on society than not. Always mouthy and trying to tell men how things should be done. Once they'd spread their legs and served their purpose, it was time to liberate them from life.

Something he was getting quite good at.

He smiled. Even those who tried to cross him were no match for his superior ability.

He sighed and stretched out on the couch, pillowing his head with his hands laced together. Plenty of time later to put his women away. The night was still young, but he had to go in early tomorrow, so now he'd sleep. Like a baby, knowing his problem was solved.

They'd never catch him.

∞

Nikki groaned and snuggled into the warm pillow. Her body felt refreshed. How long had it been since she'd slept all night with no nightmares? Since before the incident for sure, and now with this new occurrence, she hadn't thought she'd get a wink of sleep ever again.

Must be the bed. It felt like heaven. Warm and formfitting. She could sleep here for days and not ever get up. Her pillow moved beneath her cheek.

What the hell?

Through her sleep-induced haze she tried to think why her pillow would be moving. Come to think of it, it wasn't the smooshiest of pillows either, but it smelled like Eli and—

She wrenched her eyes open to an expansive bare chest. Her head was propped just above Eli's pec, his arm wrapped around her, holding her close. His hand was cupping her ass. Her *naked* ass.

The last thing she remembered was him giving her the world's best orgasm. So what? She'd passed out and he'd taken her clothes off before getting naked himself and sliding into bed next to her? Obviously. At some point during the night Eli had kicked the sheets off and here he was. All six-plus, glorious feet of him.

Not to mention the eight inches or so of morning woody standing at attention.

Nikki swallowed back the desire blooming in her tummy. What would it be like to take him in her mouth? He'd done it to her. Turnabout was fair play, wasn't it? What's good for the goose is good for the gander?

She licked her lips in anticipation of how he would taste. If she could somehow get down there without waking him...

Curling her fingers into a fist, she bit the inside of her cheek. She could do this. Nikki carefully moved down his torso. His hand tightened on her derriere and she froze.

Please don't wake up, please don't wake up.

A second later his hand slipped off and he snuffled, shifting slightly to his side.

Phew. Crisis diverted. His abs were rock hard, a testimony to his diligent workout routine.

His opposite hand reached up to scratch his chest and he twitched again. Nikki paused until he settled into sleep once more. Almost there. She smelled his musky scent mixed with yesterday's aftershave. His cock jerked and she smiled. It knew she was on her way.

She took great care in sitting up so she wouldn't disturb him, wincing at her aches and pains. God he was yummy. Tanned and muscled. Mmm, mmm, mmm, mmm, mmmmm. She was going to enjoy this even if she'd never liked giving head before. This was Eli. The love of her life, keeper of her heart, and besides, she could give as good as she got. He may not have totally gone down on her but he'd still given her a fabulous orgasm.

Supporting herself with her good arm, Nikki leaned over ever so slowly and wet her lips. A tiny drop of pre-come had seeped from the slit and she licked it off with a quick dart of her tongue. The saltiness exploded in her mouth. Eli hissed above her as his cocked jerked in anticipation, yet he still didn't wake. Must be having one hell of a dream.

She would make sure he woke to the real thing.

She lapped at the broad head, loving the power she felt.

"Uhn," he moaned and she smiled before taking the tip into her mouth and sucking.

"Holy sh-shit." Eli jackknifed into a sitting position, his eyes wide, his chest heaving. Nikki followed his cock as it moved, never letting go.

She took more of him in, sucking and slurping on his length. He collapsed back again. One hand grabbed the sheet in a tight fist, the other grasped her wrist.

Nikki bobbed her head over his shaft.

"More," he gasped and tangled his fingers in her hair, gently prodding her to do as he asked.

She did until her gag reflex kicked in and then backed off. Eli let up, then pushed her down again.

Over and over they parried like this, and each time it got easier to take more of his length. His hips began lifting as she moved down until it was him controlling the blow job rather than her. She gave up and let him fuck her mouth.

His thighs tensed beneath her breasts, and his heels dug into the mattress. He was very close. She doubled her sucking efforts, ready to taste his flood of come.

"Christ," he gritted out. "Enough."

Eli reached beneath her armpits, dragging her off his cock and up his body. She looked at him with surprise.

"As much as I like your mouth wrapped around my cock, I want to be buried in your pussy when I come," he growled.

Her eyes widened even more and her puffy, reddened lips pressed together as she swallowed.

He flipped her, taking care not to hurt her sore shoulder, and positioned himself between her spread thighs. She widened further for him. With a finger, he prodded her slit to find her wet and ready for his penetration. She sighed and tilted her head back, barring her throat for him.

Eli nearly howled in triumph. His mate had come to him. She'd opened herself up and given herself to him. And he was going to take everything she offered.

With the pad of his thumb he circled her clit, drawing more of her moisture out, zeroing in on the bundle of nerves guaranteed to make her go off like a rocket.

"Don't stop, don't stop," she panted.

He kissed her forehead. "Never."

In just a few seconds he had her writhing beneath him. "You are mine, Nikki-Raine." He entered her in one quick thrust to the hilt.

She arched her back, her breasts brushed against his chest and she yelled something unintelligible. He held himself still and waited for her to catch her breath. A first mating could be explosive and he wanted her with him all the way.

Nikki looked at him and nodded, seeming to understand that he was waiting for her to be ready.

Keeping himself levered above her in deference to her injury, he pulled out and slammed back in, catching a rhythm that had them both sweating in no time.

Nikki clawed at his arms and hooked her ankles at the small of his back. Her small cries of bliss barely penetrated. The tension built until he thought his cock would burst.

Eli leaned in to nibble along the vein running the length of her neck. It was almost time.

His balls tightened as he thrust into her heated passage. His teeth lengthened. He bit.

She screamed as the twin sensations of his bite and her orgasm washed over her. Eli slammed home one more time and tensed as his cock exploded. For what seemed like an eternity, he emptied his seed deep in her womb. Her pussy clenched around him, milking him for all he was worth. His wolf howled in success.

Her thighs squeezed his hips until they could hold on no longer. He felt them slip away to lay boneless at his side. Her hands dropped too.

Eli laved his mark on her neck with his tongue, sweeping aside the hurt and healing the small bite.

The mating was done. She was his forever. Caelan would know the minute he smelled her, as would his pack. No one would touch her, but him, again. He wanted to pump his fist in the air. Instead he melted onto her, exhausted.

Only when he sensed her inability to breathe well did he move, disengaging from her pussy. She hissed as he did so.

Eli rolled to his side and propped himself on his elbow. Her eyes were closed and her nostrils widened with each inhalation. He laid his hand on her belly and laughed when it jumped beneath his touch. She smiled and curled into him.

"Mine," he grunted.

Now she laughed and looked up at him, her eyes bright in the early morning sun pouring in the window. "Yes. Yours."

"I didn't hurt you, did I?"

"Yes, but—"

"Shit, I'm sorry." He tried to roll her over so he could get a better look at her shoulder and any damage he might have caused. She resisted.

"In a good way, E." She chuckled. "It was a good hurt. And oddly enough, my shoulder isn't really bothering me."

He grunted and pulled her into a tight embrace. "Probably the painkiller you took last night."

"Last night? I don't remember doing that."

"You wouldn't, Sleeping Beauty. You were so out of it when I came in with dinner, I had to coax that pill down your throat. You didn't even wake up when I got in bed with you."

"Ah, that explains why I couldn't figure out why you were in my bed."

"Our bed." He squeezed her until she squeaked. He loved the sound of *our bed*.

"Our bed," she whispered as if trying it out for herself. "Is this real?"

He kissed the top of her head. "It's real." And soon reality would become unbelievable. Eli sighed and rubbed her back. What would she think of him then?

Chapter Nine

Nikki heard voices in what she hoped was the kitchen. She had followed her nose to the enticing scents of bacon and coffee and now paused in the doorway. Eli stood at the sink, his back to her. Tieran sat in a chair at the table, engrossed in the newspaper. Or appeared that way until she spoke.

"I can't tell you anything else, E. I felt her fear. It was dark, she was being held tightly against a wall maybe. Something solid."

"Is it something from her past?" Eli asked. "Damn I can still smell her like she's standing right here." He sniffed his shirt and Nikki quirked an eyebrow at the motion.

Who could he still smell?

Tieran shrugged. "Maybe she's awake."

"Nah. She was zonked. She'll probably sleep a while longer."

Nikki felt rooted to the floor. They were talking about her? Unless he had another woman stashed away in the house. He could smell her?

"Hey. I asked if it was from her past." Eli still hadn't turned around.

"I said no."

"You didn't speak."

"I shrugged."

"What the hell good did that do? I don't have eyes in the back of my head."

Tieran snorted. "Caelan does."

Nikki couldn't move, watching their by-play. There was an obvious affection between them. Friendly, nothing else.

"That's because he knows the mischief you get into."

Tieran spluttered with indignation. "I do not."

"Whatever, T."

Nikki smiled and smothered a laugh, not wanting to intrude. She still felt like a stranger.

A movement caught her eye and her breath froze in her lungs. A very large dog had poked its head in the doggie door. Tongue wagging as it panted, the dog cocked its head. Her heart pounded. It did not look like a nice doggie. It looked wild, like it belonged in the woods.

She didn't remember ever hearing Eli say he had a dog. Was this a stray then? Had it wandered in following the scent of food?

Damned ballsy dog if it had.

"Eli," she whispered. No response.

"Eli," she said a tad louder.

Tieran swung around. The smile on her face was replaced by a look of worry.

"What's wrong, Nikki?" Her head cocked the same way the dog's was.

Eli turned. "Hey, sweetheart, I've made... What's up?"

Why the hell did everybody in this house cock their head the same way? Couldn't they see what she saw? The enormous dog getting ready to devour them all.

She indicated the door with a slight nod. "Don't move."

"Shit." Eli sprang toward the door at the same time Tieran stood.

"Don't move," Nikki yelled. She could see it now. The dog would leap in and attack the first available body, which was Tieran.

"It's okay, Nikki, it's just Cae—"

"Out." Eli's shout drowned out Tieran's words but Nikki could swear she'd heard the other woman say it was Caelan. Eli pointed out the door and the dog disappeared with a pathetic whine.

Why would Tieran say the dog was Caelan unless... Oh God. The blood drained from her face.

"She doesn't know yet, Eli?" Tieran's shrill voice interrupted.

"No, damn it."

"What is it with the men in this house?" Tieran slapped her thighs and marched out of the kitchen. She stopped beside Nikki. "When he's done explaining things to you, come to me and I'll explain them again. Better yet"—she smiled—"we'll go to his mom's. She's fabulous. You'll love her." Tieran's hand squeezed Nikki's in a comforting gesture, leaving Nikki more confused than ever.

Across the room, Eli heaved a sigh and dropped his chin to his chest. The outside door opened and Caelan strode in.

"Good morning, guys." He grinned. Fully clothed, not a hair out of place. No way had he just been a dog.

"She knows, you idiot, the gig is up." Hands on hips, Eli faced his brother. "Why'd you do that?"

"Like I knew she'd be standing there."

It dawned on her then. She hadn't seen a dog. "You're werewolves." Nikki hated how unstable her voice sounded. Derek had been telling the truth then. She'd believed him on some level, but really, who wouldn't have doubted him? Werewolves? And nobody knew about them?

Both men looked at her with identical grimaces.

"Shape-shifters," they said together.

Nikki spluttered and stabbed at the doggie door. "Y-you were a wolf right there. That makes you a werewolf. Oh my God."

"Nikki-Raine."

Her body trembled in fear. No, not fear, she'd heard the rumors, had joked about it, and Derek had confirmed them in the hospital. But to actually see it was just downright bizarre. So if it wasn't fear, why was she trembling? Trepidation, maybe? Concern about the unknown?

"Damn, she's just like Tieran with that werewolf bullshit. Why didn't we get normal mates?" Caelan growled.

Nikki's ears perked and she backpedaled. "Mates?"

Eli groaned. He covered his face with his hands and took a deep breath. "You wanna leave now, Cael?"

"Yup. Leaving." He stopped next to her the same as Tieran had. "When he's done explaining things, go find Tieran. She's been through this."

"Yes, thank you. She mentioned that already." She had to fight to keep from gritting her teeth.

"My mate did that?" His grin took over his face, showing his dimples.

The same dimples Eli had that made her body melt. Caelan's didn't have the same effect and she wondered why.

They were identical after all, so why didn't Caelan make her mouth water and pussy tingle?

Caelan nodded. "She's good like that."

An intense growling sounded from where Eli still stood. "Back off, brother."

"Eli," Nikki gasped. She'd never seen him act this way.

Caelan moved on, tilting his head as he went. "Don't worry about him. It's all part of the mating. It'll dissipate sooner or later." He looked back at his twin. "Dissipate, not go away." And then the door swung shut, enclosing her and Eli in the kitchen.

By themselves.

"Please don't be afraid," he pleaded.

The sadness in his voice fortified her. "I'm...not. I just, well, this is all kind of unreal, you know?"

He nodded and pulled out a chair for her. When he held his hand out to her she went as if tugged by a string. She'd never be able to deny the man anything.

Nikki sat. Eli left her side for a moment and filled a plate with fluffy scrambled eggs, bacon, a biscuit and some delicious-looking melons. She didn't know how he could eat at a time like this. Her stomach and brain churned with questions and possible answers. It was a good thing she hadn't needed to take a pain pill this morning or she might not remember having this conversation.

He yanked out the chair next to her and scooted it until the front touched the side of hers. Doing a double take, she glanced up at him.

The plate of food was placed in front of her. A fork and a glass of juice followed. She looked back and forth between the food and him.

"I don't think I can eat right now, Eli."

"You can"—he straddled the chair so his knees surrounded her seat—"and you will."

Before she could huff in protest, a long, lean finger covered her lips. "You need to eat. You're too skinny."

Tears welled in her eyes. She hadn't eaten or slept well in more than eight months.

"Hey." He lifted her chin with the tip of the finger that had sealed her lips. "It's okay. You're safe here."

Nikki blinked but couldn't stop a fat tear from rolling down her cheek. Eli swiped at it with his thumb.

"I will never let anybody touch you, Nikki-Raine," he vowed.

She sniffed and nodded. "I know." She did know, too. She believed he would never hurt her or, to the best of his abilities, allow anyone else to either. But he couldn't be with her every moment of the day. The same way Derek hadn't been able to drop her off at her friend's house that night. If he had... Christ, if he had, he might be injured too. Or worse, dead.

"Do you want to talk about it?"

The lump in her throat enlarged tenfold but she nodded. She needed to know now, not later. As if her life wasn't weird enough.

"Do you want to ask questions or just listen to me talk?" His thumb came up to brush a lock of hair behind her ear and stayed to rub the lobe.

Honestly? How the hell did she know? "This is a little overwhelming."

The soothing rub continued. "We'll take it one step at a time."

"How many of you are there?" Might as well jump in somewhere.

"Lots. Whole communities. You wouldn't know one if you saw one."

"You think?" she mocked, looking at him like he'd lost his ever-loving mind. She'd known him for how many years and didn't know? Except for the rumors... Maybe she was the one losing her mind. Maybe this was a dream and she was still lying in bed.

He smiled on a puff of a laugh. "You're not dreaming."

Her mouth fell open before she could stop it.

"Sweetheart, I didn't tell you before because we don't tell anybody. It could be detrimental to our race."

"Does Derek know?"

Eli dropped his chin to his chest and she knew she had her answer. "Yes. He's known since high school."

"But he couldn't tell me?"

"I made him promise not to."

"All those times I asked him about you and he shrugged me off. He knew all along."

"I wouldn't have told him either except he saw it happen one time while he was here."

Okay, fine. She could live with that. It hurt to know he felt he needed to hide something like this, but she could deal. On to the next round.

"Why did Caelan call his wife mate?"

Eli sighed and looked resigned. "Because they are mated."

"And that means what, exactly?"

"It means they belong to each other. Forever."

She chuckled. "You make it sound so permanent."

Eli never took his very serious gaze off her. "It is."

Oh. "But she's not a wolf...thingy."

"No. She's one hundred percent human," he agreed, ignoring the wolf-thingy barb.

"So, her *dreams* don't have anything to do with being a...werewolf."

"A shape-shifter, Nik, and no, her abilities have nothing to do with us. You'd have to talk to her grandmother about those, I believe they were passed down through her."

"Why don't you say werewolf?" Seemed a bit odd since they were, essentially, werewolves.

He shrugged. "The term werewolf had such a negative connotation in centuries past, that for the most part, we've adopted shape-shifter. It's what we do, shift into a different shape, and besides, there are some groups of shifters that change into different animals."

"Holy shit." How did the world not know about this?

"We're very good at keeping secrets, Nikki-Raine."

"Okay, you've got to stop reading my mind, it's freaking me out." As if she didn't have enough of the heebie-jeebies right now.

"I'm sorry, it's just, we have this connection between us now and your face makes it so easy to guess what you're thinking."

He leaned in and kissed her cheek. He smelled so good. Her clit tingled with the contact of his lips, and she squeezed her thighs together.

Wait a minute. "Connection? What the hell are you talking about?"

Eli moved closer until his chest brushed her upper arm. His right arm stretched out along the chair back and his left arm lay along the side of the table.

"We're mates, Nikki." His lips nibbled a path on her chin, and his breath tickled her skin.

She shivered at both the sensations on her face and his words. Mates. Her eyes slid closed and she tilted her head to give him better access with his teeth.

Nikki jerked upright, her eyes flying open. "You bit me," she accused.

He nodded. "Yes."

"Why?" She'd thought it was all part of the sex. Clearly she'd been wrong.

"It's part of the way a shifter forms their bond. By filling you with my come"—he laid his palm on her belly and she silently cursed when her pussy jumped to attention—"and marking you with my teeth and saliva, it tells other shifters that you belong to me."

He showed absolutely no remorse for biting her. A warm fuzzy feeling coursed through her. It felt good, right, to be claimed by him. Did this mean...

"Am I pregnant?" she blurted out, then winced when she realized how dumb she sounded.

Eli growled and stuck his nose into the crook of her neck and shoulder.

"No." He bit her ear gently.

"Now how would you know that?" *And furthermore, you ditz, why did you ask him as if he would know?* God what a loser she must look like.

"I can smell a conception. I can smell when you're in heat. Soon, because we're mated, your body will come to crave mine."

Too late, it already does.

He backed away to look into her eyes. His were almost glowing a gold-brown. "Mine, Nikki-Raine. No one else's. No one in my pack would ever dare lay a hand on you now, but human men won't know the difference. I can become very possessive, Nik. I think you'll find that out very shortly."

"You mean like how you snapped at Caelan a few minutes ago?"

"Yes," he gritted out.

"He's your brother, for God's sake. And his wife is pregnant."

"Doesn't matter. I won't like any man getting close to you."

Nikki took a minute to absorb Eli's words. Why the hell wasn't it bothering her to hear all this? Why wasn't she running out the door? Her heart thumped hard. The same heart she'd given to him long ago.

So what should she do? Accept what he was telling her, as unbelievable as it sounded, or think on it? Nikki trusted him implicitly. He'd proven his love for her over and over the last... How many hours had it been? Despite her scars. She also couldn't stand the thought of living without him. There was no question as to whether she'd stay, but maybe some time to process was in order.

Nikki stood abruptly, knocking her chair back and surprising Eli, whose eyes widened with her departure. She wouldn't go far. Couldn't go far. Her body wouldn't let her, but she did have to go.

Eli stood too and she noticed the slight tremble in his legs and the fear in his eyes. She started to reach for him, but pulled back at the last second.

"I need to be alone. For a little while," she said, feeling beyond stupid.

The wounded look on his face nearly ripped her heart apart. She didn't need to be alone. Didn't want to be alone. Why was she doing this? She needed explanations, not quiet time to reflect.

She shook her head. By this time tomorrow, she'd be certifiable. Too many thoughts jumbled in her brain.

"I know, sweetheart," he soothed, surprising her. He was giving her space. He didn't look happy about doing it, but would just the same. It was one of the reasons she loved him.

"I'll be here if you need me." Eli placed a gentle kiss on the tip of her nose. He turned and left her standing there staring at his back.

Need him? She needed him like a fish needed water. There was no question about that. She'd *needed* him since before the news of his ability to do an entirely unimaginable thing.

Chapter Ten

"Ah, there you are."

Nikki twisted in the overstuffed glider rocker she'd sequestered herself in. Tieran stood in the doorway. When she moved further into the room another woman followed.

"Any reason you chose this room to hide in?" Tieran raised an eyebrow.

Nikki smiled and relaxed. "Nope. Just found it when I was wandering and couldn't resist this chair."

"It's my favorite."

"The room is beautiful. Did you do it?" Nikki kept her eyes on Tieran as the other woman sidled up next to her.

"Pfft. Are you kidding? You think Caelan would let me near a paintbrush? The fumes are noxious, don't you know?" she said, rubbing a hand over her distended belly. "And a ladder? Won't even go there. I did do the directing though. Oh, and thank you."

"Aye, aye, aye." The older woman stepped forward. "My sons are big, overbearing babies themselves. Not letting a woman decorate her own nursery. What is wrong with them? My dear Nicole, I am Judith. How are you?"

Nikki felt her face redden.

"Crap, I'm sorry, Judith. I meant to introduce you," Tieran muttered.

Before she knew it, Judith had pulled Nikki from the depths of the plush chair and enveloped her in a bear hug. "Good grief, to hear Eli tell about it, you'd think half your face was missing."

The blood that had pinked her cheeks a second ago, drained suddenly. Eli had said her scar didn't bother him. Now she knew the truth.

The older woman sighed and patted Nikki's back as if she were a long lost friend. "Oh for pity's sake, don't look like that. This piddly ole scar"—she traced a slim finger down the scar's length, making Nikki flinch—"doesn't bother my son a bit. I just meant he'd said you were cut up in the crash and that I shouldn't make a big deal of it when I saw you. I was picturing your eyeball hanging down and your ear out of place."

Nikki let out the breath she held and a tiny smile tugged at her mouth as she envisioned what Judith described. She liked his mother immediately.

"It's so nice to be able to hug at least one daughter-in-law. Don't get to with this one," she said, jerking a thumb in Tieran's direction.

Don't get to? Because she was pregnant? Was Tieran the kind of person who didn't like anyone touching her belly? Nikki hadn't gotten that vibe from her at all. Or maybe it had something to do with Tieran's psychic abilities.

Suddenly it occurred to her what Eli's mother had also said.

"Oh, Eli and I aren't married."

Judith smiled. "Yes you are."

Tieran snorted. "Might as well be."

"It's all right, Nicole, I know everything. Besides, I can smell him all over you."

Nikki's stomach dropped and she barely refrained from sniffing her shirt. Mortified, she wondered exactly what Judith could smell.

"Relax, it's a wolf thing," Judith teased.

"Yeah. You know, Judith, I don't care what any of you say, it's still a little weird what you guys can smell," Tieran added.

Jesus. What had Eli said earlier? That he could smell a conception or her in heat?

Judith turned to Tieran, her face incredulous. "More weird than what you do?"

Nikki choked back a laugh.

"You got me there." Tieran sighed and plopped into the chair Nikki had just vacated. "My back is killing me."

Judith's eyes popped open. "You don't think it's labor, do you? Don't underestimate back labor. I almost did with the boys. Got to the hospital in the nick of time."

Talking about babies put more questions into Nikki's head than she wanted to deal with, but Tieran had said to ask her anything.

"So are you going to have a...um..." God, how did she put this?

"A pup?" both Judith and Tieran said together.

"Yes," Nikki said, deflating.

Tieran shivered. "God I hope not."

Judith swatted her knee. "I already told you no, silly girl."

"I know, but I keep envisioning this hairy little furball coming out of me."

Nikki couldn't help it. She laughed. Judith joined in, then Tieran. The three of them laughed until tears ran down their cheeks.

"Oh," Judith finally spoke when they'd all settled down. "Ladies, I think we should move this conversation into the kitchen where I can get a drink."

"I asked you if you wanted a drink when you got here, Judith."

Eli's mom winked at Nikki and headed for the door, throwing over her shoulder, "Not that kind of drink, dear."

Nikki snickered again.

"Oh well," Tieran said, struggling out of the chair. Nikki helped her to her feet. "I could use a Mountain Dew."

"Isn't soda bad for the baby?"

Tieran's lip curled and Nikki sucked in a breath at the fierce look on her face.

Judith returned to Nikki's side. "One thing you'll learn about Tieran, dear, is that you should never mess with the girl's Mountain Dew. I was here the night Caelan tried to talk her out of it until the baby was born." She sighed dramatically. "I'm not sure my son's ego will ever recover."

"Damn skippy," Tieran hissed. "Just because I'm carrying his furball, doesn't give him permission to run my life."

A few minutes later they were ensconced in the kitchen. Tieran contented herself with a Mountain Dew, Judith sipped a glass of red wine and Nikki drank a hard lemonade she'd found hiding amongst the condiment bottles in the refrigerator door.

"So here's what happens, since I'm almost positive Eli didn't tell you the specifics. Trust me, I had to go to Judith to get the details." Tieran shifted in her seat, looking for a more comfortable position. "A pack has a hierarchy. The top is called the Prime. He's kind of like the go-to guy for major problems, keeps the pack in order, blah, blah, blah."

Judith laughed. "Actually, there's quite a bit more involved."

Tieran waved her off. "Nikki doesn't need to know all that right now. So at one time, Caelan and Eli's dad, Judith's mate, was Prime."

"That's right," Judith proclaimed proudly. "My Liam made a mighty fine Prime."

Tieran rolled her eyes. "You'll have to excuse Judith, she's a little infatuated with Liam. You'll see. Anyway. Liam retired and now Caelan is Prime."

Nikki's eyebrows shot upward. "Caelan is king?"

Mountain Dew shot from Tieran's lips. "Lord, don't say that when he's around. His head's big enough as it is."

"Okay." Nikki chuckled. "But, if Caelan and Eli are identical twins, how did Caelan get to be k—head honcho? Did they fight for it?" She vaguely remembered watching some special where the wolves fought for supremacy.

"Nope," Judith answered. "Luck of the draw."

"Huh?"

"Caelan was born first."

"You're kidding. A couple of minutes is all that's keeping Eli from being Prime?"

"Yep. Not that Eli wants to be Prime anyway. And now"— she patted her belly—"with this little guy on the way, poor Eli's shut out."

Judith snorted indelicately. "Yeah. Poor Eli. He's probably jumping for joy. Don't get me wrong, Nikki, Eli loves his job as Second, and would take over the pack in a heartbeat if need be, but he'd rather be working his security jobs. Now with you here, he'll probably even back off of some of those. That's just how shifters are when they meet their mate."

"Hmm." Nikki bit her lip. She wasn't too sure about this whole mate thing yet. And having Eli around more seemed way too stifling for her peace of mind. A change of subject was definitely in order. "So, if you're not having a...pup, then when can they...you know, become a wolf?"

"Not 'til puberty, so I'm told," Tieran said before taking another big gulp of her soda.

Judith nodded. "Right. And there's plenty of time for you to learn all this."

Nikki was doubtful. It must have shown on her face because Tieran took pity on her.

"I was in the same boat you're in not too many months ago. It gets easier, I promise."

"I'll always be here to help too, dear." Judith was nothing like Nikki ever imagined a mother-in-law to be.

Mother-in-law? No. Yes? Damn. She bit her lower lip. They had her so flustered she was starting to think the same way. Worse, she wanted it. Wanted a life with Eli in it. Had since high school probably, but those dreams had been shattered until the last few days.

What exactly was she running from? The love of her life, who with every moment of the day was proving how much he loved her back? Why?

She realized in a shocking discovery that the one thing she'd dwelled on for eight long, agonizing months didn't matter in this house. She hadn't even thought about her scarred face until Judith had touched it with a tender finger. No one had given her the pitying looks, or murmured behind her back when she turned around. No one cared about it except her.

So how long would it take her to get over it?

Now, she decided, with resolute determination. It was part of her life, it wasn't going to go away.

"You look like you're deep in thought, dear. Anything we can help with?"

Nikki took a deep breath and wiped her sweaty palms on her thighs.

"No," she said and tried to smile. "I have to deal with this on my own, but everyone here has already gone a long way to helping. Thank you."

The only thing she had left to deal with was the guilt over losing her friends and not being able to do anything to save them. Tears flooded her eyes.

"Oh, sweetie." Judith moved and enveloped Nikki in a bear hug.

"I should have been with them," Nikki whispered against Judith's shoulder.

"With who? Your friends? Then without a doubt, you would be dead too." Tieran rubbed circles on Nikki's back.

Nikki nodded. She knew that. In the bottom of her heart, she knew Tieran spoke the truth, but it hurt. She had a feeling, years from now, it would still hurt. The only thing left to do was find justice for the lives of her friends. If she had to search until the day she died to find the man responsible, she would.

"Better now?"

"Yes." She'd already convinced herself that night in the hospital there was nothing she could do to bring her friends back. She tried to shut out the imagery, tried not to think about it. For the most part, she'd held it together. Didn't take much to bring it all to the forefront though. It would take her a long time to get over what she'd seen and stop missing her friends, but she would get passed it. Especially with these two women offering their undying support, or when she lay in Eli's arms, nestled into his warmth and protection.

After a few more minutes, Judith released her from the bear hug and held her at arm's length. Tears shimmered in her eyes.

"I have to go out of town for the next couple of days, but don't ever think you can't call me if you need to." She gave a reassuring squeeze.

"Me too. God knows I've got my own amount of guilt for what I put Eli through way back when. I still haven't forgiven myself for thinking he could have killed those... Well, we can have a pity party whenever you want. I'm a moody bitch right now anyway." Tieran tucked Nikki into a hug. Her belly made it a little awkward and the baby responded to the sudden pressure by kicking out.

Nikki laughed and wiped her eyes with the back of her hand.

She would be okay.

Chapter Eleven

Nikki was gone. The second he opened his eyes, he knew she wasn't in the room or the connecting bathroom. Eli bolted upright in their bed. Why the fuck hadn't he sensed it before now? One of their security lights flared to life outside and beamed through the slit of the curtains on the bedroom window, illuminating the empty half of the bed. Distressed sheets told him she'd obviously fought a nightmare.

Damn it. His mate had tossed and turned and he hadn't felt a thing. Worse, someone was in their fucking yard and he hadn't sensed it. Calling on all his shifter senses, he drew a deep breath. Throwing back the covers, he jumped off the bed and wrestled himself into his jeans.

He felt her now, her stress, her fear. He sensed Caelan stirring awake, and Tieran, dead to the world. No one else, though. Nikki was alone wherever she was. Unless whoever made the light come on had the ability to mask his scent. Another shifter might.

He inched the curtain back further with hands that were close to becoming paws. Through the window he saw her, standing on the small rise to the back of the house. Her arms were wrapped around her waist, and a small breeze tugged at her hair and the tail of his T-shirt she'd thrown on. Her long, bare legs stood out in the bright light of the security beam.

She looked fucking lonely as hell.

Eli strode out of the bedroom, where a very sleepy Caelan met him in the hallway. "What's up?"

"Nikki needed some air I guess." He nodded at Caelan's body. "You were planning on scaring an intruder to death?"

"Wha—?" Caelan stared at Eli like he had no clue what Eli was talking about.

"You're not wearing any pants, man."

Caelan dropped his gaze. "Hmm. I thought I felt a breeze." He shrugged. "Never know when you might need to shift. So are you saying there isn't someone out there?"

"Just Nikki."

"Oh, good. I thought with the light..."

"Yeah, me too." Eli said, already moving to the back door.

"I'm guessing she didn't take too well to what we are?" Caelan asked.

Eli paused. She hadn't seemed to be too distraught. Yeah, she'd needed some space, but his mom had told him Nikki was fine. Mostly sad about her friends and the way things were happening in her life, but fine with the mating. And with Tieran and his mom around, there wasn't anything Nikki could ask they wouldn't answer.

Hell, she only had to ask him. He wouldn't hold anything back from her now that she knew everything. The problem was getting it all out the first time.

"No. I think Mom and Tieran did a good job convincing her we were real."

"Tieran thought so too."

Eli nodded. "Go back to bed. I've got to go get my mate."

He opened the door and stepped onto the patio. Nikki had sat on the grass and was watching the landscape. Leaves rustled in the trees and somewhere in the distance a lone wolf howled. One of the Samson family, by the sound of it. He saw Nikki's shoulders tense and it made his heart ache.

He walked up to her, making as much noise as he could on the grass so he didn't scare her. She didn't turn around but he could tell she knew he was there.

"Do you want to see my wolf?"

Her head tilted slightly like she was thinking about it. "Yes." Her voice was almost inaudible.

His heart thumped. Would this be what scared her off? He didn't give himself the chance to think about it. Instead he stripped off his jeans and shifted. His body craved this moment just like it always had from the very first time he'd done it.

Bones and joints popped, elongating, strengthening. Fur tingled across his skin, teeth lengthened into razor-sharp points. His fingers and hands transformed into paws.

He stood on all fours and sniffed the air. Her scent enticed him even more in this form. Now he wanted to shift back and ravish her.

Eli padded to her and nudged her elbow with his nose. She jumped and he could hear her heart hammering away at her ribs. Her breath came in shallow pants, not much different from his own.

Look at me, he willed her.

When she turned her head, her eyes were shut tight. He licked them and whined when she scrunched up her face against his onslaught. She didn't back away though and for that, he'd forever be grateful.

"Gross."

As she spoke, his tongue slid across her lips and he tasted her.

"Ugh. Enough." She pushed him away with a playful shove, a smile lighting up her cheeks.

He came back for more, pushing against her with his head, nuzzling her arm and belly. She laughed out loud and dug her fingers into his fur. Damn but it felt good. Both to see her laughing and the scratching she did along his underside.

He plopped down next to her with a sigh and laid his head in her lap. She scratched at his ears.

"This is really, very, extremely weird. You know that, don't you?"

Eli met her gaze.

"God. It's really you in there. Your eyes are the same, and this fur"—she tugged at his shoulder—"it's the same color as your head. When you're a human, I mean." She continued to pet him. "I'm talking to a dog."

Eli growled low in his throat.

"Whoa. Sorry. Wolf. I'm talking to a wolf. Because it's okay to talk to a wolf, right?"

Resting on her thigh, his nose was close to her pussy. He smelled the arousal emanating from her. She might not realize she was turned-on but he did and he wanted her. Time to end this.

His fur was like silk in her fingers and tickled her bare thigh.

Crazy.

She had to be insane to be sitting here petting a wolf. She wanted to cry with the lunacy of it all. The man she loved with every fiber of her being had just turned into a wolf. His golden eyes seemed to stare straight into her soul. A lump knotted in her throat.

Eli's wolf body began to vibrate beneath her fingers. Nikki stretched her hand out where it lay on his shoulder. Whether she was comforting him or not, she didn't know.

Incredibly, his fur started shrinking. His long snout shortened, the pointy ears receded.

Scared, Nikki pulled back. She didn't move away, but she couldn't touch him. His large paws transformed into fingers. She heard joints and bones pop and cringed at what must be very painful. Her heart broke. How did he do this? How often did he do this?

Seconds later, Eli's head replaced the wolf's on her leg.

"Jesus," she whispered in awe.

He smiled and rubbed his nose on her thigh. His hand rested on the inside of her leg just below his cheek, and long fingers stroked her skin. Nikki closed her eyes and absorbed the sensation. She loved when he touched her and lately he had his hands on her most of the time. Almost as if he thought if he stopped touching her she would disappear.

Nikki mentally snorted. She wasn't going anywhere and turning into a wolf wasn't going to chase her away.

"Are you following me?" she asked softly.

He squeezed her thigh. "I can't be apart from you for very long. Something in our wolf make-up prevents it."

She smiled. "That might get kind of awkward when I have to use the restroom somewhere."

He reached for her hand and kissed along her knuckles. "Yeah, well, I guess you'll just have to pee before we leave the house."

Nikki laughed. "And I guess you'll be the one cleaning up the mess."

"Then we won't leave the house."

"I'll get bored."

"I'll think of ways to keep you occupied," he growled. His eyes gleamed with wicked intent and her pussy pulsed in reaction. She could imagine all the ways he'd keep her busy. From what she'd experienced so far, staying in might not be such a hardship.

"I want you now."

She nodded as his fingers crept beneath the hem of his T-shirt that was three sizes too big on her. It smelled like him though and she'd needed a piece of him wrapped around her. If he felt empty without her by his side, so did she. Wearing his shirt had seemed the appropriate thing to do.

"I need to taste you, Nikki-Raine. To make love to you. To forget about everything else for a little while, except what it feels like to be deep inside you."

She swallowed. Her nipples hardened into tight buds and rubbed almost painfully against the cotton covering them. Her knees separated of their own accord and she was powerless to stop them. Nor did she want to. Eli lifted himself into the vee of her thighs and got comfortable on his stomach. Her heart rate soared seeing his head nearly nestled at her apex.

With a hand on her belly, he gently pushed her to the ground, still ever careful of her wound, and raised his shirt to uncover her mound.

"I love how fucking good you smell," he said, leaning into her core and inhaling. His shoulders pressed on her inner thighs, widening them even more and his hands came up under her ass to cradle her. On his elbows, Eli stared at her pussy, which contracted at the intensity she saw plastered on his face.

"Oh God," she breathed. She wanted him so bad. Only two measly inches separated his mouth from her labia.

A heartbeat later, nothing stood between them. The tip of his tongue curled the length of her slit, spreading her moisture and making her throw her head back.

He zeroed in on her swollen clit and she bit her lip to keep from screaming in rapture. Held captive by his hands, she could do nothing but endure the onslaught.

Nikki moaned and rolled her head on the ground, fighting off the rise of an orgasm just below the surface. She wasn't ready yet. She wanted more time to feel.

His hands kneaded her butt cheeks, drew her closer. He alternated from slow, long, teasing licks, to short, quick stabs of his tongue. It was too much. Her body tensed and he pulled away.

"Nooo," she cried, and her body arched. She tried to regain contact but he eluded her efforts. "Please. Please!"

One hand disappeared from her ass and she whimpered. The next second she sucked in a breath when two long fingers slid deep into her pussy, gliding easily on her juices.

"I could eat you all fucking day." His voice sounded guttural. Eli resumed lapping at her.

Nikki pumped her hips against his mouth. With the dual assault of his fingers and lips, her orgasm spiraled out of control. It flamed to life and flicked along every nerve ending in her body. Her heels dug into the ground, her thighs squeezed around his head and shoulders, and she fisted tufts of grass in her hands.

On and on it rolled through her, perpetuated by his incredible tongue until finally her body slouched to the ground. Still he licked at her and when he pulled his fingers from her slick folds, her nerve endings quivered with mini explosions.

Breathing heavy, she lolled her head to the side. Exhausted, she could barely look at him.

He crawled atop her body, drawing the shirt up to uncover her breasts. He kissed each one reverently, giving them equal attention. His lips covered hers.

"My turn." The amber color of his eyes glowed when the security light shut off.

Not even the sudden darkness drew her gaze from his. On his knees, he cradled her legs in the crooks of his elbows and spread her wide. The head of his cock nudged at her entrance making her gasp as nerves shot to life.

Her hole stretched to accommodate his cock, sucking him into its heat. Sweat dripped from his forehead to plop on one of her breasts. Nikki's breath hissed from her lungs as he pressed into her.

He'd never felt anything like it. Not with any woman before. They were made for each other, fit perfectly. Her thighs tightened when she bore down with her vaginal muscles, squeezing his cock in an exquisite hug. A climax loomed and he'd yet to move.

Deep inside where the tip of his cock touched her just right, he held himself rigid. Sheer willpower kept him from slamming into her pussy. And then she moved again. The tiniest of spasms in her womb and Eli lost it.

"Fuck," he ground out, shaking his head against the riot of nerve endings firing along the length of his cock. He dropped his head nearly to her chest. With a gargantuan amount of effort, Eli withdrew completely.

Nikki's beautiful eyes turned to his in question and need.

"I'm not through with you yet, sweetheart." He rose, releasing her legs, which fell open on the grass like wet noodles. His superior eyesight allowed him to see the glistening lips of her pussy. Her scent wafted to his nose making his canines explode in his mouth.

"Get on your hands and knees, Nikki." The low growled command made her eyes widen. He heard her sharp intake of air, and she swallowed before submitting to him. Every cell in his body responded.

She dragged her body into position, scooting back even, and placed her sexy-as-all-get-out calves alongside his. Her ass wiggled in front of him, grazing his cock, making it bob in excitement.

"Does this hurt you?" he rasped. He didn't know what he'd do if she couldn't take him this way. Cry, go mad, something, but he wouldn't hurt her. She responded by brushing her sweet little butt against him again.

"Be still." Eli swatted her ass with an open palm and caressed the red mark left behind. She yelped and her body jerked. He settled her with a hand on the small of her back. His nostrils flared. Another smack, this time to the other cheek, and she jumped again, but remained silent. A quick swipe through her gloriously displayed pussy juices said she liked being spanked.

She mewled and pushed back on his finger, nearly impaling herself with it. He chuckled.

"You like being spanked, sweetheart?" He already knew the answer, the proof was leaking onto her thighs.

"Unh." She rested her forehead on one arm, probably taking the pressure off her shoulder, but the action also brought her ass up in the most provocative way.

With his thumbs, he spread her cheeks, rubbing circles into her flesh and inching closer to the rosebud aperture of her back hole. She squirmed and moaned. Eli bent over her and nibbled at her neck.

"One of these days, I'm going to fuck you here," he said, pressing the tip of his thumb just past the tight ring of muscles. Her body quivered, her back arched into his chest. He bit lightly on the tense flesh of her shoulder.

"Please take me," she begged.

"You want my cock in you, sweetheart?"

"Jesus," she groaned. "I know you're a fucking man. Cut the talk and fuck me."

His chuckle turned into a growl when she wriggled her backside against his erection. If she wanted to be fucked, he'd accommodate her.

Her pussy was drenched from her orgasm and her excitement. Using his fist to guide him, Eli slid the head of his cock up and down her slit. She whimpered when he spanked her with his free hand. When she stretched, his tip disappeared inside her body.

He shuddered with her. Watching part of him merge with part of her made him want to howl at the moon. Inch by inch he pressed into her tight pussy.

Eli held still when he'd penetrated her completely. Her palms pounded the ground, her fingers opening and flexing. His wolf roared to the surface. Fucking his mate this way when he'd never had another woman like this made him lose control.

He pulled back and thrust home, slamming into her so hard she moved across the grass. Nikki threw her head back and screamed into the night. A wolf howled in the distance, answering her call as if she were one of them. A distant part of his brain recognized the other wolf but paid no attention. Not when his mate was on her hands and knees, rearing back to meet his fierce thrusts with her own in a primal dance.

Her small breasts swayed and he itched to touch them but held her hips captive instead. If he moved, he was afraid he'd lay them both out.

His balls drew up as his orgasm neared. He licked his lips at the enticing array of smooth skin waiting for his teeth. A second before his cock exploded, Eli sank his teeth into the flesh at the base of her neck. She screamed as his bite spurred her release. Her pussy contracted with what felt like a thousand tiny fingers on his cock. Sweet blood flooded his tongue as he bonded them further, mixing his saliva into her system. Every time he did this he ensured her safety as his mate.

His come flooded her womb. As he licked the mark he'd left to heal it, he cursed the fact she wasn't in her heat. For the first time, he wanted a child. Wanted to see Nikki swell with his baby. His body rocked on hers. He wanted to ring every ounce of come from his balls, wanted her to receive everything he had to give.

Lungs heaving, Eli gently settled Nikki's boneless body on the ground and wrapped himself around her, being careful not to withdraw from her body. They couldn't stay here long, not with the grass against their skin. They'd be itching like crazy in no time.

A small sigh escaped her lips. "Is this your way of treating insomnia?"

Eli tucked a few sweaty strands of hair behind her ear and kissed her cheek. "Did it work?" He'd do anything that kept her demons at bay. If it meant fucking her senseless whenever she woke from a nightmare, he was happy to comply.

She smiled and turned into his forearm. "I think so."

They laid there until Nikki shivered as the sweat dried on their bodies.

Chapter Twelve

He sat in his car and watched as the two little lovebirds nestled, and wrestled, in the back of the boy's old, beat-up sedan. She hadn't changed in the months he'd watched. Shy, demure, pretty. He could drop innocent from his original list. It was more than obvious she was not. In fact, he could take shy and demure off also. Apparently those attributes were only for public consumption. In the waiting room where he'd first seen her, she'd been all those things. But no, she was just like any other cunt.

What he was witnessing at the moment proved it. What's more, it showed just how pussywhipped the boy was. Which made him useless. He hadn't planned on taking an extra, but this kid had to go. He'd have to work him into his plan. No doubt about it. The last thing men needed was a diluted specimen among the ranks.

They were perched back in a clearing in the woods commonly used by teens for just this purpose. The same place they drove to every Monday night like clockwork. Many a good show they'd given him. He could have made a fortune taping them and posting them on the Internet, but he hadn't wanted to chance them finding out someone was watching them. He smiled. Soon, their waste-of-oxygen lives would end.

He'd do the boy first, fast. Get him out of the way so he could enjoy the girl alone. The boy would make his "male" list as his first, the girl his twenty-seventh. He licked his lips and rubbed at his rapidly approaching hard-on. Would the kid fight him? Would it be as gratifying to take a boy? He snorted. Probably not this lame-ass kid.

Tall and gangly, the boy had gotten out of the car and into the backseat at the girl's command. She needed a new routine, really. Every night it was the same thing. She made him go down on her, then spread her legs and bade him forward. A couple of times the kid had looked like he really wanted reciprocation in the oral department, but she'd shake her head and point to her pussy. Every time the boy gave in, rolled a condom on, shoved his dick in her hole, pumped a couple times and came into his rubber. Pussywhipped. A man had to take control of a woman. Make her do what he wanted even if she said no.

They would probably be easy to overtake and thus wouldn't be much fun, but after the excitement at his last hit he needed a break.

His cell phone bleeped loudly from the console between the seats, interrupting his thoughts. No. He didn't have time for this. He checked the caller ID. Fucking work.

"Yeah," he barked. He hated this goddamn cell phone, but in his normal life, people needed to get ahold of him quickly. Annoyed the shit out of him.

He partially listened to what the caller had to say, all the while watching the girl and boy fumble around in the backseat. Amateurs. He snorted softly. His fingers itched as he thought about joining them. Make it a threesome? The idea had some merit.

The caller quit speaking and he answered curtly, "I'll be there in thirty." He disconnected, threw the phone down and glared at his latest game. "Fuck." His plans for them would have to wait. He hated being thrown off his schedule. Which is exactly what that cunt Nicole had done. At least he'd gotten rid of her in a timely manner. If she hadn't fucking intruded, he wouldn't have had to risk getting caught the way he had.

Traffic was sparse this time of night, but he still managed to hit nearly every fucking red light. Too bad his real-life responsibilities took time away from what he really loved doing. Grinning, he ground the leather steering wheel beneath his palms.

His normal, everyday life sucked. Except for the fact he made a decent amount of money and lived in a house far better than the one he'd grown up in. The car was a definite upgrade too. In order to keep those things he had to earn a living when he really wanted to play all day. But what more could a man ask for? He even had the cock to go with it. Some men did not.

Feeling his dick stir, he laughed out loud to no one.

Tapping the wheel, he considered where he'd grown up. The shitty, rat-infested neighborhood had been poor back then. It was still the same today. A place no child could ever hope to escape. Its poverty-stricken grasp was too wide.

But somehow he'd done it. Blown off his whore of a mother who'd never said a positive word to him his entire life.

The light turned green and he sailed through it. Thinking about his mother had deflated his burgeoning hard-on. Bitch. The light at the next intersection turned red and he had to stop yet again.

She'd been his first; the reason he'd started the game in the first place. Oh, it had evolved over the years as he'd learned, but the absolute rush he got whenever he killed another one never went away. He'd progressed from simply following a girl home and ending her life to choosing his victims carefully, planning down to the last detail what he wanted to do and executing his scenario in a meticulous manner.

For years he'd done just that. Until that bitch ruined his last job. She'd put a hex on him or something because tonight his work had interrupted him. Something that had never happened before. Nicole had thrown him off-kilter. He'd have to work on getting back into his groove. Thinking about how he'd killed his mother often helped. Left him feeling an innate sense of satisfaction.

He could see her clearly in his mind. Her eyes had widened in surprise when he'd walked into their run-down, five-room house, his new car parked out by the curb. She'd taken in the expensive watch on his wrist and the suit that fit his well-muscled body perfectly.

He'd laughed in her face when she'd begged for whatever drug he was selling, then paced the confines of the tiny living room as he'd caught her up on what he'd been doing. She was still the same person. Still drinking herself into oblivion.

Immediately she'd wanted money from him. "Just a little," she'd pleaded.

Sitting at the interminably long red light, he smiled the same feral smile he'd given her back then.

He remembered crouching in front of her kneeling, begging figure and burning two hundred-dollar bills with his lighter, right in front of her eyes.

She'd spit on him. "You stupid son of a bitch. You never was good for nothin'. I shoulda aborted you when I had the chance." When she'd put her hands on the floor to brace herself to stand, he'd stepped on them to prevent her.

Carefully he'd reached for the half-empty bottle of whiskey and poured the contents onto her back. She'd screamed, berating her worthless, piece-of-shit son, spittle shooting from her mouth. He'd flicked the lighter again and held it in front of her eyes.

The sudden silence had been deafening. The flame had danced in her dull eyes.

"What're ya doin', ya jackass? Lemme up!"

"Go to hell, Momma," he'd growled softly. With a flick of his wrist, he'd touched the edge of her ragged shirt with the flame. Immediately the whiskey-laden cloth caught fire and with a whoosh, she'd been engulfed. He'd let her hands go then and watched as she staggered to her feet, howling in fear and pain.

She'd careened off the walls of the tiny house. The wallpaper, yellowed and stained with age, had caught fire as quickly as her clothes. Eventually the shrieking had stopped and her body had slumped to the floor with a thump. Her skin melted off her face and he'd watched with complete indifference.

Slipping his hands into his pockets, he'd leaned against the doorframe and watched the ball of fire consume his childhood dwelling, mesmerized. It had been exhilarating. And not a bit bothersome.

Somewhere in his focused attention, sirens broke through. He remembered thinking, "Hmph. Someone had actually called the fire department." He hadn't thought anyone would even bother in that neighborhood. Not with as many shootings and drug crimes that happened on a daily basis.

In the long run, the place had burned to the ground, destroying any evidence with it. No one had connected the man he was with the son he used to be. He'd never even been contacted and informed of his mother's death. Such a shame.

A horn blared behind him, jerking him back to reality, and he realized he was sitting at a green light. Somehow he'd made it through the last several lights in an almost unconscious haze. Looking in the rearview mirror, he saw that he didn't even remember driving the long stretch of Chestnut Street.

He shrugged. Just as well. He pulled into his numbered parking spot. Someday soon he'd be first. As it stood, he was high enough on the totem pole to get out of work for a few days when he needed to without questions, to play his games. It wouldn't be long before he was at the top of the pole.

He smiled and got out of the car. A smudge of dirt marring the black finish caught his attention. He stooped to rub at it with his finger before striding into the building, whistling.

ভ৯০

"We need to talk about something, E."

Eli glanced up from his paperwork. "What's up?" His twin had a bizarre look on his face. Resigned almost.

"I just talked to the detective assigned to Nikki's case."

A sick feeling filled Eli's stomach. "Tell me they've found the fucker," he gritted out.

Caelan plopped into the chair across the desk from Eli. "No. Well not the murderer." He waved Eli off. "I'm talking about the detective in charge of her attack eight months ago."

The pencil snapped in his fingers with an angry crack. To say he was a tad pissed about the bastards who'd done so much emotional and physical damage to Nikki-Raine was the understatement of the century. "What did he have to say?"

"They think they have them in custody."

"And?"

"And they want Nikki to come down to identify them," Caelan answered.

"Shit."

"Yeah."

"Did you explain to them why she's out here in the first place?" Eli dropped the two halves of the pencil and pushed them around absentmindedly. He wasn't even sure Nikki-Raine would agree to go face-to-face with her old attackers. And damn it, he'd come too far with her to set her back now.

"I did. He promised to talk to the detective in charge of that case so they could work something out."

"There's nothing to work out, Cael. I'm not putting her life in jeopardy for those pea-brains. They'll have to do it some other way. Webcast or pics or something."

Caelan nodded. "I told him that. I don't want to put her out there any more than you do, E."

Eli relaxed in his ergonomic chair. He trusted his brother implicitly. Neither one of them would do anything that might harm their mates. "Fine. Get 'em to send me a lineup and I'll have her look at it."

"It's already on its way."

"Then why the hell are we having this conversation?" Eli rubbed a hand over his face. Was it just him, or were they going around in circles?

"That's only part of the problem."

The dread returned.

"If it is them, she's going to have to testify against them."

"No fucking way."

Caelan sighed. "They killed a woman this time, E. Without Nikki's testimony they might get away with it."

Eli saw red. His fangs lengthened, ready to explode right along with the rest of his wolf. The urge to tear the bastards to bits nearly crushed him. "If the cops know they killed this woman, they don't need Nikki." No way would he subject her to a public trial for nothing.

"There's no evidence. Just hearsay. If they can get Nikki to tell what happened to her, it will set the stage. Tell the jury that they've attempted to do this before."

"He's right, Eli."

Eli stood at Nikki's words, shoving his chair over in his hurry. Caelan twisted also.

"How long you been standing there, sweetheart?" Damn, but she had a way of tempering even his worst moods.

"Long enough." She sauntered into the room, her belly peeking out beneath the hem of her shirt.

Eli licked his suddenly dry lips. His cock hardened as it always did in her presence. If she'd walked in here before Caelan had, he'd have laid her over his desk and buried himself inside the tight heaven of her pussy.

She stood at the edge of his desk and lifted her chin, her eyes daring him. "I have to do this, Eli."

"No." He shook his head. "Hell no."

"Yes."

"I'm not going to fucking argue with you on this, Nikki-Raine."

She snorted.

Eli's eyes widened at her blatant disregard.

"It is my life, Eli. I...*need* to do this. So I can put it behind me once and for all." Her gaze dropped to his desk. "And if they've killed an innocent woman like they almost did me, they can't be allowed to get away with it."

"Something else will come to light, Nikki. I'm not risking—"

"It's not up to you."

Eli charged around the corner of the desk nearest to her. "It is goddamn—"

She pressed her fingers against his lips and shook her head. "It's not."

Caelan rose. "I think I'll just go check on Tieran."

Neither one of them saw him leave.

Closing his eyes, Eli took a deep breath and held it. He released it with a whoosh, but it was another few seconds before he could look at her again. Little minx.

"I have to get over my fear, Eli. I should have done more when it happened, but I took the coward's way out. Now I have to live with the fact that they've killed someone." She stabbed at her chest with her thumb. "I could have prevented that if I had just been a bigger person back then."

"No," he said, grabbing hold of her hand and pulling her to him. "You did everything you could at the time, Nikki. This is *not* your fault."

She gave him a sad smile and whispered, "But it feels like it is."

Fuck.

How could he deny her when he knew in his heart what she had to do? It went against every protective instinct of his being.

"Damn," he sighed, hugging her to his chest. His fingers tangled in the black sea of her hair and he kissed the top of her head.

She let go of his hand and wrapped her arms around him. Her belly pillowed his growing erection, making him think of more important things they could be doing instead of arguing.

"Are you always hard?"

See? She was thinking the same thing.

Eli swayed with her. "Wouldn't be very useful if it was soft all the time, would it?" He kissed his way down her hairline to her ear and nibbled the soft flesh, inhaling her delicious scent.

Nikki cocked her head, giving him access to her neck. As if she could deny him. Tumultuous thoughts still knocked around her head. No matter what Eli said, if she'd sucked it up all those months ago and given a better description or some more details, then that woman might not be dead right now. And she wouldn't feel this inexorable amount of guilt. She shouldn't be making out right now. She should be at the police station picking out faces.

Eli's tongue lashed out, licking her from tender shoulder to earlobe, making her shiver. The man had one hell of a talented tongue. Talented enough to make her forget everything for a moment. His lengthened teeth nipped at her throat and her knees went weak.

If he wasn't holding her up, she'd probably hit the floor.

"I could take you on my desk right now," he growled, sending a whole new set of goose bumps parading down her arms. "I can smell your arousal, sweetheart."

"Mmm." Any kind of rational response fled. His hands wandered over her fevered body, down her sides, around her butt cheeks, up her ribcage, surrounding her breasts.

Before she knew it, he had her top off and his fingers were plucking at her nipples.

Eli rotated, turning them so her butt brushed against the edge of the desk. His mouth devoured her, laving her face and neck to her chest and the soft flesh there. She needed to feel his skin, to run her fingers over his abs. Nikki pulled at his T-shirt, tugging it from his waistband. She slipped her hands beneath and smiled when he hissed in a breath.

She knew from the rock-hard cock against her belly that he was more than ready to take her, just like he'd said.

With his hands cupping her ass, Eli lifted her and set her on the desk. He brushed the papers off by sweeping his arm across the top. Nikki attacked his button-fly. The buttons weren't easy as strained as they were over his cock.

"Damn, I can't wait to be inside you. Hurry."

"Impatient pup." She laughed when he growled.

"I don't see no pups around here. Yet."

Nikki's breath caught and she lifted her head to look at him. His eyes glittered with desire and...hope? He wanted a child? She'd heard him call some kids pups at one time, and why not? They were the children of shifter parents, would someday be able to become a wolf themselves.

"Yes, Nikki, I want a baby with you. Lots of them." His dimples deepened.

She swallowed and imagined her belly big and round with his baby. Hell yes, she wanted the same thing.

Nikki attacked his buttons with renewed fervor. The third one was stuck. He flipped her fumbling fingers out of the way and tore the fly open. His cock sprung free and she wrapped her fingers around his velvety length.

Eli leaned forward and rested his forehead on hers. "Harder," he whispered, his eyes closed, his tongue dipping out to lick his lips. A glistening drop of pre-come seeped from the slit. Nikki used her thumb to spread the moisture. His cock jumped when she hit a nerve-filled area and he gritted his teeth.

"Damn that feels good. Fuck," he grunted when she twisted her hand up and over the head.

"Stop." Eli pulled back. "I'm gonna come all over your hands and I want to be buried inside you first." He pushed her back until she was lying on the desk and slowly unzipped her jeans.

His warm hands slid into the top of her panties and pried the material over her hips, taking the jeans with them. He stripped off her pants, leaving her naked and panting. His cock jutted proudly.

Eli kneeled before her and spread her thighs. Nikki scrambled to prop herself on her elbows.

"Relax."

"I want to watch."

His eyes widened and glowed, his nostrils flared.

She wanted to watch but couldn't because the minute his tongue touched her pussy, her head dropped back and her eyes closed. Small delicate licks became long swipes from her anus to her clit. Nikki dug her heels into the side of the desk, her thighs quivering.

Within seconds he had her begging. He sucked at her clit but not with quite enough pressure for release. She whimpered. His tongue lashed deep inside her and she squeezed his head between her legs.

She glared at the top of his head. "Please," she cried.

Eli lifted his gaze to hers. "That's what I wanted to hear." He smiled and inserted two fingers into her channel, scissoring them so they caressed her inner walls, nearly making her jump off the table. "So wet," he crooned. "Mine."

His tongue returned to her clit, flicking and torturing it until the nub was ready to explode. At the last second he pulled it completely out of its hood and pressed the tip of his tongue to it.

Nikki's entire body seized. Tingles shot to her curled toes, and her nipples throbbed. Head flailing back and forth, she slapped at the desk. It was the most intense orgasm she'd ever had. All the while Eli assaulted her with his mouth and fingers, wrenching every last drop of the orgasm from her body.

He rose after she stopped shaking, a grin splitting his face.

"My turn." His voice was guttural. Eli stepped between her thighs, lifted her legs around his waist and placed the plum-shaped head of his cock at her entrance. The most tender look crossed his face. "Are you ready?"

Nikki nodded. "More than." She reached both hands up and laced her fingers with his. Tieran had told her that shifters could sense when a woman was ovulating. Was this one of those times? Could Eli sense her heat, so to speak? She didn't think it was, but obviously a shifter's nose was more reliable than a calendar.

He pressed in, inch by delectable inch. Her body bowed off the hard surface as she took all of him. When she glanced to his face she could see his control slipping. Sweat dripped from his forehead to land on her belly, and his neck muscles corded.

"Go," she invited.

Eli let out the breath he was holding and withdrew. Then she knew nothing but the pounding of his hips on her inner thighs and the drag and thrust of his cock in her pussy. He bent forward, bracing his hands on either side of her. In this position his pelvis struck her clit.

His lips covered a nipple and sucked it deep. She moaned at the dual sensations engaging her system.

It didn't take long. A minute later, the beaded bud of her breast popped from his mouth and Eli stiffened above her. His hips shot forward, pushing her across the top so far her hair dangled off the other side. A couple more inches and it would be her head.

Long spurts of his hot come drenched her pussy. He held her to him with a bruising grip on her hips as every last drop was wrung from him.

Breathing heavy and still imbedded deep inside her, Eli collapsed onto her belly, his head beneath her chin. They lay there in silence until her tailbone protested the weight of his body and the wood beneath.

"Eli," she whispered and nudged him with a weak hand. "Can't breathe here."

"Breathing is overrated," he mumbled into her breast.

"Well then, my ass hurts. Get up." She shoved but her noodly arms did nothing.

"Grr. Okay." Finally he stood, pulling out of her sheath at the same time. The action rasped her inner tissues, wrestling another round of pleasant tingles from her core.

He swatted her thigh and helped her to a sitting position. His gaze never left hers.

Only a stupid, unfounded, lingering fear of his rejection kept her from blurting out, "I love you, Eli."

Chapter Thirteen

"Do you recognize any of them, Ms. Taylor?"

Nikki's entire body shook uncontrollably. Even with Eli standing behind her, grounding her and smoothing his hands up and down her arms, a shiver dominated her senses.

"Nikki?" Eli asked, leaning over to whisper in her ear.

Her heart hammered, she could barely take a breath.

"Breathe, Nikki-Raine."

She could smell the stench of the second one in line's breath, feel his calloused hand pressing against her mouth, his erection digging into her hip. His name was Marco. "Push her between the cars, Marco," number four had said. Number five had to be the one who'd been leaning against the van. The one with the raspy voice who'd said, "Hell yeah, I wish I had me some ass like that."

Cold glass slammed into her cheek. Her keys stabbed into her chest. Where was everyone? Why was no one coming to help her?

"Nikki." Eli's near shout jerked her out of the memories she'd lived with night after night in her dreams. Seeing them in the flesh brought it all back. She swallowed.

"Ms. Taylor?"

Nikki nodded. "Yes." A tight, comforting squeeze on her shoulders followed her answer.

"Great. Can you tell me which ones?"

She turned and looked at the detective. How many times had she spoken to him all those months ago? How many times had he practically begged her for more information? Some of those times he had made her feel more like a suspect than the victim.

"What happened?" she asked.

He shifted his stance to one foot, a manila folder clutched across his chest. After a deep breath he said, "The same thing that happened to you, only this time, the victim died."

"How did you catch them?"

He breathed out heavily again and she wondered why he didn't want to tell her. She was the one going to help put them away, and had been their *victim* too, there wasn't any reason to not give her the details.

"A witness saw the victim running from them about a half hour before the crash and from evidence on the victim's body."

Nikki seethed. "What was her name?" Eli's thumbs rubbed tiny circles on the muscles she knew were hard as knots in her shoulders. He was careful to stay away from the wound.

"What?" Clearly, the very easy question had flustered him. His cheeks puffed in and out and a dull red painted his cheeks.

Anger suffused Nikki. "What. Is. Her. Name?"

"Well, I don't see how—"

"Nikki asked you an entirely reasonable question, Detective Starks."

The detective's lips formed a thin line and his nostrils flared. Almost huffy, he flicked the folder open in front of him and peered at the papers inside.

"How can you not know her name?" Nikki hissed. The thumbs moved to the base of her skull. "She's not just a victim. She was a person, a woman, with a family. How can you help her if you don't even get that involved?"

"Ms. Taylor," he defended himself, "if I let myself get that involved I would take every case home with me."

She closed her eyes. Part of her knew he was right, but it still rankled that he seemed to have no remorse or care for the woman these three men had taken the life away from. As a cop it was his job to protect. In her opinion he couldn't do that well with such complete indifference. When she opened her eyes again, she didn't see any remorse on his face. He still didn't care.

"Her name."

"Claire Simmons."

Nikki turned back to the very bored-looking lineup of six men standing opposite the one-way glass. Three of them had attacked her then left her to die in the carnage of twisted metal that had been her Jeep. They deserved everything they had coming to them, and she would gladly do her part to put them away.

"Two, four and five," she said.

"You're sure?"

"Positive."

"It's been more than eight months, Ms. Taylor."

Damn condescending man. "Were you a woman in a past life, Detective?"

"I fail to see how that's relevant."

"Were you a woman in a past life?"

"If I were you, I'd answer her." Eli's stark voice made the detective's jaw tic.

Eli's warm hands moved down to cradle her waist. Nikki wanted to lean into him, let him take her weight. She didn't though. Any sign of weakness would let the detective think he'd won.

"No," he gritted out.

"Then you've never been attacked by a group of men, forced to submit to something vile and then run off the road and left to die, have you?"

He looked down at the ground.

"Have you?" she asked again.

"No."

"Then believe me when I say that you tend to remember things like facial features and smells and...and names. Penis sizes even. The way his hands felt smashed against your lips, or the pitch of his voice. You never forget the way number five laughed in the background like raping me would be the most fun thing to do in the world. Or how number two's name is Marco, because that's what his friends called him when they wanted him to push me between the cars. You never forget the rasp of a voice."

Eli's hands had tensed immeasurably on her hips as she spoke, and a low growl emanated from his chest. The detective probably couldn't hear it but she was so in tune with Eli now, she could. His canines would most likely have descended in his mouth, growing longer and sharper in anticipation of a hunt. She'd learned so much about him and loved him more than ever before.

"You'll probably never know the feeling of being trapped in a situation you can't get out of. You'll never face nightmares night after night of being attacked by three men twice your size. Trust me when I say, 'I'm sure.'"

He stared at her for a long moment. The dead quiet in the room suffocated her. Her head spun and she thought, if it weren't for Eli holding her up, she might sink to the floor.

"Fine. I'll have some paperwork for you to sign and then you can meet with the DA. He'll have some questions for you."

"Then he'll have to come out to the house. Nikki shouldn't be here any longer," Eli said over his shoulder as he took hold of her hand and led her to the door.

The detective spluttered. "But—"

"But nothing. I let her talk me into bringing her here thinking it might give her some closure on that part of her life. Staying here will only add to her exposure and I'm not willing to do that. In case you've forgotten, those thugs"—he stabbed a finger at the lineup—"aren't the only thing she's a witness to. And if history's anything to go by, I'd say your killer is a hell of a lot more of a threat to her than those bastards."

Detective Starks lifted his chin. "I don't know what you're talking about."

"You wouldn't," Nikki said. The detective was so wrapped up in keeping himself from getting too close to the victims, he wouldn't know one if they jumped up and bit him in the ass.

"Let's go, sweetheart." Eli yanked open the door and stepped into the hallway. They weren't going to get far. Detective Morales stood against the opposite wall, waiting for them.

He smiled and pushed off the wall. "Ms. Taylor, Mr. Graham." He held a hand out to shake.

Only Nikki's fingers on his chest prevented Eli from howling into the air.

Fuck.

Morales retracted his hand and patted his thigh.

"Well. I heard you were going to be here today and I wanted to give you an update on the case."

Nikki took an anxious step forward. "What is it?"

"We're leaving," Eli said at the same time.

Nikki swung around, hurt flooding her face. His shoulders sagged. She made him feel like he'd just flushed her favorite goldfish down the toilet. Alive.

"What?" he barked at Morales, never taking his gaze off her watery eyes. He only had to think about her sleepless nights trapped in dual nightmares and he'd relent to anything. His little minx smiled and turned back to the detective.

"You'll have to excuse him. I had to pull his hair out by the roots to get him to let me come at all."

Morales relaxed. "Totally understandable. If you were my wife I wouldn't want to let you out of my sight either." He started walking.

"Out of your sight is one thing, out of the house is another." Nikki followed the man, leaving Eli to bring up the rear.

The detective glanced at Eli, an eyebrow perked.

"He's the protective sort, I see that. You're perfectly safe in the precinct though, you know that, don't you?"

Nikki nodded. Eli grunted. "That's what they say at post offices across the country."

The statement earned him a glare from Morales and a backhand to the gut from his mate. His breath whooshed out.

What? Fucked-up people pulled guns and went on shooting sprees in some of the "safest" places on Earth. Churches, schools, courts. The fucking police station wasn't immune just because cops could fire back. Eli wasn't about to let the man who'd shot Nikki get off that easy.

"Have you remembered any more?" Morales asked.

"Detective, it isn't a matter of remembering more. I've told you that a hundred times. I didn't see anything but my..." She stumbled in her words. Eli wrapped her in a hug from behind.

He fucking hated this. Hated seeing her scared to death when she used to be the most carefree woman on the planet. Now simple little noises made her jumpy.

She inhaled. Her soft breasts rose above his arms. "There's nothing but dark-colored hair and black clothes. His head was down so I didn't see his face, and I didn't take the time to look at him while I was running for my life."

Morales searched her face for a moment then nodded. "Right." He resumed walking.

When they reached his cubicle, he offered them both a seat. Eli gently pushed her into one as Morales spoke. "You mentioned a boyfriend before. Can you tell me anything else about him?"

Nikki's head fell back. "No. Nothing more than what I've already told you. I hadn't seen my friends in person in a long time. I had talked to them a few times and I know Amy and Kelly both thought he was strange, but that's it. I can't even tell you what he looks like because I've never met him."

"Neither can we," the detective said, exasperation clear in his tone. "Did you know your friend had absolutely no pictures of her boyfriend in her house? There's nothing to even suggest she had a man in her life. It must not have been an exciting relationship."

Eli watched Nikki bristle at the implication. Her best friend was dead. Not just dead but savagely murdered and the police were questioning the woman's love life?

"Maybe they weren't serious," she hissed. "I. Don't. Know."

"Nikki, he's only trying to find the guy. Any information you have might help," Eli consoled. "Maybe one of your friends said something that stood out to you."

She swallowed and her gaze searched his. "I think his name is Jim, or John. Something short with a J. And..."

Morales lifted an eyebrow and sat forward. "Yes?"

Nikki shook her head. "I don't know. It might be...no, it's probably nothing."

"How about you let me decide that."

Eli gripped her hand in his. He had a feeling in a minute she'd leap out of the chair and strangle the detective.

Her fingers squeezed his back. "Fine. I remember Lou telling me at some point about J-man leaving every once in a while."

"Leaving how?"

Nikki shrugged. "You have to realize I was under a lot of different painkillers at the time. I think she talked about him being kind of flighty. Like he would ponder things, or his mind would just wander away sometimes. She also mentioned him leaving town on a couple of occasions. Wouldn't tell her where or when he was coming back, just that he'd be gone a few days."

Eli felt her palm begin to sweat against his. Her knee started to shake in a nervous twitch.

"That's all I know, Detective, and like I said, I might be making it all up. I could have been hearing things."

Morales nodded and made a notation in his notebook. "Gives us a starting point at least. Meanwhile we've got someone watching her house in case he returns." He folded his hands on his desk. "Our profiler says the guy's very precise.

He's working on determining what type of work he might do." He shrugged. "Maybe that'll help."

Nikki stood, her bottom lip quivering. "Great. But I don't give a flying fig if the man is a neurosurgeon or a janitor. He killed three of my good friends." A fat tear rolled off her cheek to plop on Eli's hand.

He stared at it as if it were burning him. In a way it did. Every tear she cried tore at his heart. It was his job as her mate to make sure she was happy. He was failing.

"Find him," she spat.

Nikki turned and stormed to the door, her shoulders back. He could tell she was trying hard not to lose it in front of the detective.

Eli snarled at Morales before jumping from his seat and following Nikki out. She had paused in the hallway and was wiping her face with the back of her hand. He enveloped her body in a tight hug just as she sniffed.

"I'm sorry, sweetheart. If I knew who did this, I'd rip his limbs off."

Soft laughter slipped from her lips and she nodded. "I know."

He had to get her out of here. Take her home and fill her mind with other things. She'd done her job here today, much as he hated bringing her here.

Nikki was silent as they walked to his car, but shocked the hell out of him the second they were sequestered inside.

"I love you."

For several wild heartbeats, all he could do was look at her red, puffy, tear-stained face. His cock roared to life. She'd said it. They were already bonded for life, but hearing her say those words sealed it completely for him.

He swallowed. "You can't say that when we're in a car, Nikki-Raine."

A silly grin lit up her face. "Why not?"

"Because I don't have enough room to fuck you here." He started up the car. It would take them half as long to get home as it did to get here.

She laid a hand on his thigh, making his cock jerk beneath his zipper.

"Damn it, Nikki-Raine. Not in the car."

"I've never done it in a car."

He could almost hear the pout in her voice. His teeth lengthened into razor-sharp points.

"You should be damn glad you haven't 'cause if I had found out, I would have killed the bastard."

She snickered and he relaxed a miniscule amount. Distracting her worked in keeping her mind off her dead friends.

Eli trapped the hand wandering dangerously close to his rampant cock. Whenever he felt her tugging on it, he tightened his fingers around hers.

"You gonna hold my hand all day, or what?"

"I'm gonna hold it until I can get you in the house."

"And then what?"

"We'll try to make it to the bedroom."

Her laugh cut short when a flashbulb popped in her face through the window. A reporter tapped the glass and shouted, "Ms. Taylor. Are you here because of the murderer? Do they have a suspect?"

"Son of a bitch." Eli's curse overrode the squeal of tires as he whipped out of the parking space, nearly mowing the reporter and photographer down.

Nikki screamed next to him and buried her face in her hands. Eli pushed her down with a hand on the back of her head.

"I goddamn knew we shouldn't have come here."

Un-fucking-believable. The reporter charged after them as if they held the key to the mysteries of the universe, a microphone held out in front of her.

Eli punched the steering wheel, ignoring the pain flaring over his knuckles.

Nikki sat up and twisted in her seat to look back, then turned to him, her eyes filled with horror. At least she knew the monumental effect this could have on her life. She was supposed to be dead to the world, not off gallivanting in public.

"Oh, God. I'm sorry," she whispered.

Eli's breath hitched in his throat.

"I can protect you, Nikki-Raine. Never doubt that."

She nodded and took his hand in a death grip. "I know."

Somehow he managed to steer with the hand she still held—which dragged her across the seat closer to him—and fumble with his phone.

"What are you doing?" Nikki snuggled into his side where he felt her body tremble.

"Trying to find out who sold you out."

She jerked upright. "How do you know—"

"No one knew we were coming, Nik," he growled. "The only fucking way that reporter showed up is if someone pointed them in the right direct— Morales," he barked. "Find your fucking leak before I do, or so help me God, you'll have a cop killer on your hands." Not that they'd be able to prove anything beyond a wild animal attack anyway.

Nikki hissed and her fingers tightened on his arm in warning. He shrugged it off. Nobody was going to mess with his mate.

"Right. That's why there was a goddamn reporter waiting for us to come out."

He paused to listen to the bunk Morales fed him and to get on the highway. They couldn't get far enough away from here.

"You better hope to hell her face doesn't show up in tomorrow's paper.

"Yeah. You do that." Eli slammed the flip shut and tossed the cell onto the dash.

Nikki sighed. "I'm sorry," she said again, sinking into his side.

Fuck.

He wrapped his arm around her and held on for dear life, renewing his vow that nothing would happen to the woman who held his heart in the palm of her hand.

ര❦

"No. No, no, no, no, no." He scrambled for the remote and hit the volume button. Her face took up the top right quarter of the sixty-inch screen, big as day and minus the bullet wound to the head.

He threw the remote at the wall. It slammed into a mirror, shattering both the plastic casing and the glass before falling to the floor with a thud.

"Motherfucker." Still alive. And she'd been at the fucking police station according to the background image. The cameraman had done a good job capturing her surprise through the window.

He'd been played. His own fault, really. A better man would have made sure. Gone to her funeral and opened the casket, cut out her heart, eaten her liver. Something. Instead, he'd fucked up and believed the fucking cops. Like there was a million reasons to trust anything the cops said.

Now he knew the truth. All this time he could have been doing something about the bitch and here he was, sitting back and luxuriating in the process of finding a new player. The thrill of the hunt was what it was all about.

They'd denied him that right. Taken away from him the one thing he cherished. He'd have to scrap his plans for the teenage couple and find where the cops had stashed little Ms. Taylor.

He dragged a pen and paper from the drawer in his kitchen and sat down to make a list. Lists were good, kept everything organized and handy. He liked lists.

First things first, find a mole. Someone on the police force he could use to rat out her whereabouts. Second, scope out the place they thought was safe enough to keep him out. Third, eliminate the target.

He smiled and sat back in the chair, folding his arms across his chest. He'd take the weekend to find the stuff he needed and make his move Sunday night. He had Monday off, so things would work out perfectly and he'd have the extra day to come off his high.

His cock hardened beneath the scrubs he still wore, tenting the material beneath the tie. He chuckled at it. "Greedy little bastard, aren't you?"

He loosened the bow and stood to let the pants fall from his hips. The slit glistened with a drop of pre-come. Imagining it was Nicole Taylor's mouth he fucked after binding her, he wrapped his fist around his cock and pumped. He'd have to add this scenario to his list. Fucking her mouth, ramming his cock down her throat while she could do nothing to prevent it.

Just the thought of her face shoved full of his dick, tears streaming out of her eyes, her nose running, made his balls draw up. Two pumps later and thick streams of his semen shot into the air. His knees shook as he continued to stroke himself, wringing every last drop out of his cock.

Damn, he couldn't wait.

Chapter Fourteen

"How did you do this?" Nikki whispered, staring at the computer screen with tears running down her face. Her arms were crossed tightly over her chest, and her fingers dug into the skin just above her elbows.

Eli sighed. Standing behind her, he massaged the tension in her shoulders. It was the least he could do after not being there for her all those months. He shrugged, knowing she couldn't see the action.

"It's what I do, baby. Surveillance, security cameras. It wasn't hard to set up a closed-circuit TV for this. I know you wanted to be there and I'm sorry you couldn't be."

Her legs wobbled, threatening to collapse, so he left her to wheel the chair closer. He pushed it to the back of her knees and further, forcing her to sit before she fell. Without a word, she took his offering and propped her arms on the desk. Chin in the palm of her hand, Nikki watched the funeral of her best friends.

"They were so fucking young," she choked, and a fresh batch of tears flooded her face.

Eli retrieved a box of Kleenex and set it in front of her. A lump formed in his throat. He wished on all the stars in the sky she didn't have to go through this.

"All this time I've been hiding when I should have been spending time with them."

He rubbed between her shoulder blades. Nothing he could say would make this any easier for her, but he tried. "You were only doing what your body and mind allowed you to. You aren't a coward, and even if you had spent this time with them, it still would have happened." He didn't mention how she most likely would be dead also.

Nikki blew her nose and leaned closer to the screen. A woman stood at the podium, reading a eulogy.

"I should be doing that." With a shaky finger, she pointed to the screen. "That's supposed to be me. I've let them down," she wailed.

Eli's breath hitched. *Damn that fucker to hell.* He knelt beside his mate. Comfort was the only thing he could offer outside of hunting the son of a bitch down and killing him. Doing so would leave Nikki unprotected and no way in the world would Eli allow that to happen. Maybe if Caelan didn't have other duties and imminent baby worries of his own, but it didn't matter. For the moment, Eli had to trust the police enough to do their job.

"Oh, God," she cried.

Eli looked at the monitor. Another casket was being carried in. A woman's cry echoed throughout the church. Nikki laid a finger on the screen, stroking the woman's image.

"Kelly's mom," she mumbled. "She must hate me."

God damn it. "Come here, Nikki-Raine." He wrapped his hand around the back of her head and pulled her to his shoulder.

Her body shook with heaving sobs and sniffles. Eli held her through the letdown. She needed this more than anything. Wouldn't do her any good to keep it bottled up. He soothed her

155

with slow caresses the length of her spine and murmured assurances in her ear.

"I love you, Nikki." He kissed her temple as her body began to settle. The fury would come again, no doubt, but for now she seemed to be quieting. "We will find the bastard who did this. I promise."

It was a promise he wouldn't break. One way or another, if he had to search until the day he died, he would find the asshole responsible for causing Nikki so much pain.

She nodded against his shoulder, a silent sort of trust in him.

The door clicked open behind Eli. Nikki stiffened in his arms. Eli turned. Caelan stood in the doorway, a solemn look on his face. He hitched his chin, beckoning Eli over. Eli gave a short incline of his head before kissing the top of Nikki's head and squeezing her in a tight hug.

"You okay?"

She sniffled and nodded again, then drew away from him. Her face was splotchy red, tracked with tears. He thrust a Kleenex at her before rising.

"I'll be right back."

She didn't respond, and he didn't expect her to. He moved away.

"She okay?" Caelan asked, drawing him into the hall.

"No." He turned and watched her. She bit her thumbnail and stared at the screen. Even from this distance he could see the sheen of tears in her eyes.

"Detective Morales is here. He wants to talk to you two."

Hearing the urgency in his voice, Eli swung his gaze back to Caelan.

"She's watching the funeral," Eli hissed. "Now's not a good time."

"I think you'll want to hear this, E."

Intrigued, Eli dropped his shoulders. "Fine."

He followed Caelan to where his brother had left Morales standing by the front door. The detective held his hand out and Eli accepted.

"What's going on?"

Morales grinned from ear to ear. "It's over."

"What?"

Eli spun at Nikki's stunned gasp behind him. He hadn't even realized she'd followed them. Opening his arms, Eli coaxed her to join him. She didn't hesitate. He enfolded her in a hug and tilted her face up to drop a kiss on her lips. Her face was still a marbled red color and her nose ran.

"How?" she croaked.

Morales shifted his stance. "We've been staking out the house, waiting for this mysterious boyfriend to show up. He finally did."

"Are you serious?" Nikki asked.

"Yes." The detective smiled again. "Got there late last night. We arrested the suspect and brought him in for questioning. You were right about the J. His name is Josh Summerton. He's been begging for his lawyer and he's got a rap sheet a mile long. Rape, burglary, even had a restraining order slapped on him for stalking a woman. Plus, he has absolutely no alibi for the night of the murders. Says he was in a hotel room all alone."

"But did he do it?" Eli growled.

Morales shrugged which didn't make Eli feel a hundred percent better.

"There was no evidence at the scene. Pinning this on anybody is going to be difficult, but I'm confident we've got him. Crime Scene unit has been swarming his house all night and morning. We pulled his records and have people looking at his computer. The phone is clean. It's like he doesn't use it. We even found several pre-paid cells at his place. He's done a lot of traveling, has weekends blocked off on his calendar, and he's one meticulous son of a bitch too, by the looks of his apartment. But here's the clincher. He's a nurse at the hospital. How the hell he ever got a job as a nurse is something we'll be looking into, but we suspect he's been using an alias."

Eli fisted his hands, one of which got tangled in Nikki's shirt. She drew in a sharp breath and her body went rigid beneath his arm. Nikki turned into him and buried her face on his chest, sobbing.

"We'll know more tomorrow and I'll give you a call then, but for now, I think it's safe for you to relax your guard a little. This guy is looking like our prime suspect. And hey, if you were innocent, wouldn't you be all over the 'I didn't do it' speech? Not a word out of this guy," Morales said, popping his gum.

Eli shook the man's hand. "Thank you." If his breathing came a tad easier, no one needed to know it but him. Now he'd be able to concentrate on Nikki and their future.

Everything seemed to be happening so fast. First the three shitheads had been arrested and now this. Eli cocked his head as he watched Morales climb into his unmarked squad car. How in the hell was it possible this was all coming to a head?

Why the fuck was he questioning it?

"It's really over?" Nikki turned her face up to his.

He idly played his thumb over her shoulder. "Looks that way," he muttered. If only he could get rid of the nagging feeling it wasn't.

ఆర్ఠ

A shrill ringing made Nikki jerk in his arms. "Shh," he quieted her and rolled out of their bed. The clock glowed a red 6:28 in the morning. Eli snatched the phone from his nightstand and pushed the talk button before it could ring again.

"Graham," he said softly, not wanting to disturb Nikki. He turned back to her. She'd rolled onto her side. The creamy expanse of her back and buttocks beckoned him to return under the covers. His cock hardened.

"I need your help over at the Stanton's. They're having trouble at the border again," Caelan groused.

"Jesus. Couldn't they have waited until a reasonable hour?"

"Tell me about it. I've been here since five."

"Fuck." Eli swiped a hand over his face and looked at Nikki again. Her shoulder rose and fell with each soft breath. He didn't want to deal with anything else other than sleeping with his mate right now.

"Yeah," he grumbled. "No, we'll be there as soon as we can."

"Not we, E. You're better off leaving Nikki at home," Caelan said.

Eli paused, waiting for his brother to elaborate on why. When he didn't, Eli asked, "What do you mean leave her here?"

"Things might get ugly, E. You don't want her in a dangerous situation."

No, he didn't, but he also wasn't ready to leave her alone. "God damn it. Fine," he hissed after a minute, and slammed the phone into its base.

Nikki screeched and reared up. Her hair flew in a crazy tangle around her head. For a second, Eli forgot about what had to be done. He smiled at the untamed look of his mate. If it weren't for the fact her eyes were sleep-hazed, he would swear they'd just had a wild romp between the sheets.

"What happened? What's going on?" she practically yelled.

He chuckled at her struggle to join the ranks of the living.

"I have to leave," he said through clinched teeth.

"Oh. Okay." She flopped onto her pillow and snuggled in again. "Later."

Eli snorted. "Don't get so upset, huh?"

"What do you wan' me to say, E? I'm tired. Your fault. Get lost."

He came around the bed so he could see her face. "I want to take you with me."

"No."

Eli bent and placed his palms on the bed a foot away from her body so he leaned over her. "Excuse me?"

"No."

He gritted his teeth and counted to ten. "Get your pretty, little, smart-ass butt out of this bed and get dressed."

Nikki opened one eye and stared at him. "No." She turned her face away from him and yanked the covers over her head.

Exasperation filled him. He tugged on the blanket. "I don't have time for this, Nik."

"And I don't have time for you badgering me when I'm trying to sleep," she mumbled under her shield. She whipped the covers off. "If you had left me alone at all last night, I wouldn't have this problem. Now, shoo." Her eyes slid shut, blocking him out.

"Damn it, Nikki-Raine. I don't want to leave you alone."

"Why not?" she groaned. "Morales said everything was safe now. Go, save the world or whatever it is you werewolves do."

He growled low in his throat. "Just because he said it was, doesn't mean I'm going to take any chances."

"I won't leave the house. You can call me every ten minutes if you want."

His growl turned to a snarl.

She sighed. "It has to stop sometime, Eli. I can't live in hiding forever. If the police feel confident, then I guess so do I."

"Damn it. I hate it when you're reasonable."

"Me too. G'night."

"What if I *want* you to come with me?"

"That's a misguided attempt at making me feel guilty so I'll come with you and therefore be safe in your eyes," she muttered.

Eli stood. Son of a bitch, she was a stubborn woman. He chewed on his thumbnail as he watched her sink into sleep once more. Could he do this? Could he leave her here without him or Caelan?

Caelan was probably worse off than Eli anyway with Tieran being so far pregnant. He wondered how much shit Cael's mate had given his twin before he'd left in the early morning hours.

His shoulders dropped. At this second, pack business took precedence. If Morales hadn't told them the news earlier, little miss tiredness better believe he'd have packed her in the car. He scrambled for clothes, showered and dressed in less than ten minutes.

"I love you." Eli kissed Nikki's temple.

"Uh-huh. Nove oo too," she said into her pillow.

CR&O

Nikki stepped out of the shower onto the fluffy bath mat and wiggled her toes in the softness, delighting in the feel of it. It had been too long since she'd indulged in such a simple pleasure. Way too long. The amount of time she'd spent hiding in her parents' house to be exact. And here she was doing the same thing at Eli's. Hiding. Well not anymore.

Somehow she'd gotten Eli to actually leave the house this morning without her. He'd called a few times, thank God it hadn't been every ten minutes like she'd suggested he could. Talk about overbearing. For the first time in a long time she felt safe from the intrusions of the outside world. Not even the news broadcasting her face a couple nights ago had dampened her spirits.

Okay, it had. Big time. Then the funeral had done a good job of bringing them down even further. But now it was over. Nikki felt guilty for the tiny bit of giddiness flowing through her. Why should she get to be happy when her friends were dead?

Eli went a long way in redirecting her thoughts whenever he saw them leading in the wrong direction. Her clit tingled in reaction to how he handled her depression.

Besides owning their own security business and genuinely knowing how to protect her, they were wolves. She considered that an added advantage. Nikki smiled, remembering the furry beast snuggled up to her outside in the grass the night she couldn't sleep.

At first, she'd been shocked, but then, when she'd looked deep into those beautiful golden eyes, she'd known it was him and her fear had disappeared. She'd felt none when he'd shifted back into his human form either. He was who he was and it only made her love him more.

After towel-drying her hair, Nikki stood in front of the foggy mirror and surveyed her naked body. The red, angry scratch on her shoulder ached with memories both raw and ugly. The jagged scar across her cheek seemed to pulse, forever reminding her of the past. Eli didn't care about her looks or what had nearly happened to her that stormy night.

Suddenly, she didn't either. Since coming to his home, she hadn't even thought about her face. Well, except when his mom had brought it up, but afterward she hadn't tried to hide it or hide from it. *Eli* made her feel that way. His perception of her hadn't changed because three men had tried to rape her, leaving her feeling dirty and sorry for herself. Instead, he'd *claimed* her to use his word. She bit her lip. Nothing could top the way he looked at her like he wanted to devour her. She had no reason not to believe him when he talked of their future together. Especially not after meeting his mother and hearing Tieran.

Her heart thudded and she gripped the towel in one hand while wiping the mirror with the other. A fat drop of water fell from her eyelash. She tried to look deep inside herself but all she saw was her reflection.

With shaky fingertips, Nikki ran her fingers atop the faint bite mark marring her shoulder. She still couldn't believe he'd bitten her. Nor that he'd done it more than once and she didn't care. Not when he had his cock embedded deep in her pussy and her clit screaming for release.

She wished he were here to help dry her off. There wouldn't be much drying happening with his insatiable cock throbbing just inches away, but it would be fun foreplay.

Shaking off the vision of him bending her over the counter and taking her from behind was a delicious effort. She yanked her toothbrush out of the holder and squeezed a dollop of toothpaste on it. For the first time in all these long months she finally felt in control of her destiny. A destiny she had thought gone for good.

Nikki wiped again at the mirror, smearing her image with the condensation gathered there. Outside the bathroom she heard the click of the bedroom door opening and a pained voice call out.

"Nikki?"

Shit. Tieran sounded more than desperate. Nikki threw her T-shirt over her still-damp body and hurried through the door to find out what was wrong. She stopped short when she saw the fear etched on Tieran's face.

"Eli's gone too?" Her teeth were ground together, her lips pinched so tight they were white, and her eyebrows were scrunched together.

Please God, don't let her be having this baby. What the hell could she do? She didn't know anything about babies other than they smelled sweet, cried a lot and pooped.

Nikki crossed the room with long, quick strides. "What's wrong, Tieran?"

Not the baby, not the baby.

"The baby. It's coming."

Son of a...

Nikki grabbed hold of Tieran's arm when she slumped against the doorframe and doubled over as a fresh wave of whatever seized her. One of Tieran's hands reached out and captured Nikki's forearm. Ragged fingernails dug into her flesh.

Nikki's eyes rolled and she bit her lip to keep from shouting in pain.

It seemed like an hour before Tieran's grasp loosened and blood flowed once again into Nikki's hand. She flexed her fingers to aid the process. Slowly Tieran righted herself using the wall next to her as leverage. Her pale face blended in with the white walls.

"Where is that hairy-assed bastard when I need him?" Tieran wailed.

Nikki bit back a smile. Tieran was one tough cookie but she would never call her mate a hairy-assed bastard if she wasn't in so much pain. Well, at least not behind his back. She might say it to his face. Or was she talking about Eli?

"Umm...Caelan?"

"No," Tieran ground out. "He had to go to some pack thing in the middle of the night. Where's Eli?" she growled on another wave of labor pain.

Shit. This was bad. Very bad. "I believe he's at the same thing. I think Caelan called him earlier this morning." Damn why hadn't she woken up enough to listen instead of arguing because she'd wanted to go back to sleep? Both of them were hairy-assed bastards.

Tieran's nostrils flared with her deep intake of breath. "It's coming so fast, Nikki. I think we need to go." Tears welled in her eyes. "No one ever said it would be like this. I thought I would have a long time, all day, all night. Oh my God, I'm going to have this baby here at the house."

"Tieran!" Nikki yelled. "Take a breath, honey. Breathe." She motioned with her hand in a circle. Dumb jackasses, leaving her here with a hysterical pregnant woman. Who did they think she was, Wonder Woman?

Nikki left Tieran standing next to the door and hurried around the room, dressing in whatever clothes she could find. Her bra stuck out from beneath the bed where Eli had flung it last night, one sock had landed on the lampshade, the other across the room on the arm of the big chair, and her jeans...where the fuck were her jeans?

She swung her gaze over the room. There, hanging on the doorknob of the closet door. In a moment of insanity, Nikki cocked her head and raised an eyebrow. How the hell had they managed to get there? Yanking the jeans off the tenuous perch, she ran to the dresser and pulled out a skimpy pair of underwear.

"Umm, okay, how far apart are the...contraction thingies?" Her underwear refused to cooperate with her warm moist skin and Nikki nearly left them off.

A tiny smile creased Tieran's lips. "About ten minutes, I guess." Her voice wobbled.

An alarm went off in Nikki's brain. Damn. That was pretty close together, wasn't it? How far apart were they supposed to be, and shit, how close together would they get at the last second? She battled with her jeans, hopping on one foot to try and get the second leg on.

"But my water broke twenty minutes ago, and since Caelan was gone I came to get Eli."

Nikki stood, her lungs heavy from the exertion of getting dressed quickly, and stared at the almost unflappable woman Nikki knew Tieran to be who was now in tears.

She was so going to kill Caelan. And Eli for that matter for leaving her with a heavily pregnant woman.

Nikki held up a hand when Tieran's lower lip quivered. "Never mind. We can do this, Tieran. We are two grownup, capable, able-bodied women and somehow we will do this." She snapped her fingers and raised one in the air. "I'll call Judith. She can meet us at the hospital." Eli's mother would know exactly what to do. Hell she'd done it with twins. Feeling rather proud, Nikki inhaled and relaxed. Everything would be fine. She would call Judith right now.

Tieran shook her head. "She's out of town, remember?"

"Oh, for the love of..." Nikki plopped down on the big chair and jerked her socks and tennis shoes on.

"I think we'll have to go alone, Nik. I know you're not supposed to leave the house, but..."

Nikki held up a hand. "Wait just a minute. I don't think they planned on having an emergency birth, do you? You're what two, three weeks early? Caelan wouldn't have left this morning if he'd thought you were going to go into imminent labor. Of course I'll go with you." She stripped her arms out of the T-shirt so the cotton hung loosely over her chest, and wrapped her bra around her. After catching the clasp together in the front, she twisted it until the cups were covering the appropriate tiny mounds of flesh that really didn't need a bra and slipped her arms through the straps. A second later she was both completely dressed and discombobulated.

Raking her hands through her hair, she rushed into the bathroom and thrust her deodorant under the shirt, swiping it across her underarms for the barest amount of coverage to get her through the day. Perfect.

"I still don't want to put you in any danger. Trust me," Tieran murmured. "You don't want to put your faith in the wrong person."

"You saying I can't trust you, woman?"

That earned Nikki a semblance of a smile, even though she knew exactly what Tieran was referring to. A certain cop who had turned on the pack and betrayed every one of them, ultimately landing Eli under arrest for a large list of felonies including murder. The whole thing still made Nikki see red and she hadn't even been around then except as a friend.

"Eli is gonna be pissed," Tieran said with a sniff.

"Yeah, well Eli should be here then, shouldn't he? Tieran, look, if he's mad, I'll deal with him. Morales said I was safe, I have to believe that right now. I hardly think Eli or Caelan would want anything to happen to you or the baby. Now, if your water broke already, isn't it like really close to time?" Nikki reached out and took hold of one of Tieran's hands. "I don't know nothin' about birthin' no babies, Tieran, and I really don't want to."

Tieran nodded. "Okay."

"Besides, we'll be at a hospital. What could possibly happen there?"

"You don't really want me to answer that do you?" Tieran asked, coming to a stop as Nikki pulled her out the door.

"No." She didn't need to answer. Nikki remembered all too well what could happen. But they'd caught the guy, right? "And besides, no one will know I'm there today, will they?" She hoped. "I'll put a hat on if that makes you feel any better." She'd have to try and convince herself she had nothing to worry about.

Tieran's gaze searched Nikki's face and she held on to the stoic look, wanting to convince her they would be all right. After a brief pause, Tieran agreed and they were off.

"I'll call Eli on the way and have them meet us there. Since they're at the same place, they can come together," Nikki said over her shoulder.

Chapter Fifteen

Eli snatched the phone from the console. Two more minutes and he'd be home. His chest was tight with anticipation, that's all. Not something else. Certainly not a feeling of dread like the shit was about to hit the fan. Nikki was safe at home and the pack business had been handled smoothly. An issue over a boundary line had turned into a squabble that had taken both Caelan's Prime abilities as well as Eli's Second.

He could taste Nikki already. The feel of her firm, budded nipples on his tongue, the velvety softness of her skin, and he was hard as a rock beneath the button-fly of his jeans.

The caller ID window displayed "one message". His eyebrows came together. How the fuck had he missed a phone call? When he'd been pumping gas? He was just about to flip the phone open to see who'd called when its shrill ring filled the car. The message was replaced with a number he recognized and the feeling of apprehension slammed into him full force.

There were only two reasons Morales would be calling and one of them sucked.

"Morales, what's up?"

"We've found our leak."

Make that both of them sucked. Eli sat up straighter from his slouched driving position. "And?"

"And he admitted to tipping off the press about Ms. Taylor being at the station. His ass is about to be fried, trust me."

"You better hope you get to him before I do."

"He's already been gotten to, Mr. Graham. Caught red-handed. That's not all."

Eli's heart slammed against his ribs, threatening to break them at the implied threat. "What the fuck's going on?"

He heard Morales' sigh. "This cop had a bit of a gambling problem. We discovered he's done this sort of thing more than once to make a little money on the side. Apparently he's been a go-to mole for a while. Somebody needs something covered up, he's the man. Need some info, he'll be there for you."

"So?" Eli asked when Morales paused for a second too long. He wanted to strangle the detective for being obtuse.

"He was contacted Saturday, looking for information on Nicole Taylor."

"Son of a bitch." The car swerved wildly to the side. Eli fought to control it, taking the phone off his ear so he could steer with both hands. If that cop was a shifter, he was a dead one.

Eli heard Morales repeating his name as he pulled onto the shoulder and brought the car to a shuddering halt.

"You there?"

"I'm here." *Seeing a red haze, but I'm here.*

"He rolled on a lot of information he'd given out in exchange for a plea bargain for a lesser sentence. He says he feels guilty for getting Nicole's picture on the news and figured with the timing of this guy's request, it had to have something to do with the news report."

"You think?" Eli yelled into the phone.

"You know, I'm not happy about this situation myself. It's my witness he's dipping in the grease."

"I don't give a shit about your witness, she's my mate."

There was a silent pause he could have cut with a knife and Eli realized his mistake.

"Mate?"

"Yes, mate," Eli growled, "as in I love her and she's stuck with me forever." Hopefully his quick thinking would divert the detective's attention.

"Ah. I see. I didn't realize you two were that close."

Damn. Eli blew out a silent breath and hung his head, wiping the sweat from his brow. Not in his entire life had he slipped about what he was until now.

"We are," he said wearily. "I would give my life to save hers."

"I see. Then keep her away from doctors."

Eli jerked his head up. "What the hell are you talking about?"

"It wasn't the boyfriend," Morales said gravely.

Motherfucker. He knew he shouldn't have left her alone this morning. He wanted to scream. He wanted to shift and tear something apart. "How do you know?"

"The reason he was out of town was because he was meeting with his parole officer in another state. He shouldn't be anywhere near here but it seems as long as he showed up for his scheduled meetings, no one thought to check up on him."

Morales continued, "We've learned some things through the profiler involved in the case." Eli heard the shuffling of papers. "He thinks the killer does have some sort of medical background."

Eli straightened in his seat. "Then he could still be an employee at the hospital."

The detective audibly sucked in a breath. "That's a hell of a leap, Mr. Graham."

Eli shook his head. "How can you say that? He knew we were at that hospital."

"So did the rest of the world," Morales said dryly.

"He knew enough about her to find her there."

"Probably wouldn't have been hard."

"And he knew when she was leaving. He fucking waited for her," Eli insisted.

A sigh was his only reply.

"We didn't tell anyone we were leaving and were, in fact, very careful in getting her out of there. So you tell me. How in the hell could he have been there waiting in that wing without having been there all along and watching us? If he worked there, he would have blended right in and not caused suspicion in anyone."

"You're right. I totally agree with your assessment, however, do you know how many medical employees work at that hospital? Do you know how many hospitals are in this area?"

Eli sat forward. "It's your job to look into each and every one of them."

"Don't tell me how to do my job."

"I wouldn't dream of it," Eli snarled.

"Look, our profiler has tagged him as being in the medical field. This idiot contacted our leak on his cell phone. We're in the process right now of triangulating the signal. When we find out where he called from, we'll have a better idea of where to start looking. All I'm saying is keep Ms. Taylor close for a little while longer until we find this guy."

"I won't let her out of my sight." *Again.* "Let me know when you get something." Damn this would kill Nikki. This morning he had a strong suspicion she was ready for freedom. From her confines and her fear.

"I will," Morales answered.

Eli slapped the flip closed. "Fuck," he shouted and willed his heart into a normal rhythm. He was about to throw the phone into the passenger seat when he remembered there was a message he needed to check.

He opened it again and followed the commands to retrieve the message. According to the time stamp he'd missed the call almost thirty minutes ago. Nikki's harried voice hit him like a sledgehammer between the eyes and made his heart pound.

"Tieran's in labor. Had to take her to the hospital. We called Derek to meet us there. Tell you more later. Love you. Oh, and we're fine. I'll make sure to stay with Der at all times just for you. Bye."

Eli's gaze flitted between the phone and the road, disbelief making his blood run cold.

Surely she had not just said what he thought she said. Please God, tell him she wasn't on her way to the hospital.

He tried to swallow past the lump in his throat, his entire desolate future without Nikki-Raine passing in front of him. Bile rose and he forced it back. Spots swam in his vision. He'd never make it there in time.

CZ80

He dropped his chin to his chest the minute he saw the bitch. She stood next to one of the curtained-off ER cubicles. His heart thumped and he nearly spilled the black sludge some of his co-workers referred to as coffee. Next to him, the first-year resident he'd been walking with droned on. He tuned the kid out.

Fuck her for being here and disrupting his inner sanctum, his world. Stupid, stupid female. Since the moment he'd seen her face on the TV he'd searched for her and gotten nothing. Not even his mole had been able to track her down. He cursed the day he'd missed his golden opportunity. The sun, the angle, the back windshield had all prevented him from severing her head from her neck with a well-placed, high-caliber bullet. He wouldn't even think about the fact he'd missed her the first time either.

He curled his lip in disgust. Slicked over by the fucking cops. He still couldn't believe it. They'd put one past him, big time, and here she stood, plain as day, her gaze traveling apprehensively over his ER.

Bitch.

His hand cramped around the ceramic mug, making him realize how tightly he gripped it. Taking a deep breath, he calmed himself.

Nicole Taylor was nervous. With good reason. The last time she'd graced the halls of his hospital, she'd been shot. And then he'd shot at her again. Maybe what he needed was a day at the shooting range. His skills were a mite rusty, it seemed. Of course he'd never really practiced on a moving target.

Her hands twisted in front of her abdomen and she continued to search the area with wild eyes.

Had she seen him? Could she identify him somehow?

No. Not possible, and even if she thought she could, no one would ever convict a respected doctor. Plus, if she'd been able to identify him, he wouldn't still be standing here.

An agonized scream split the usual hubbub of the ER. Nicole jumped and disappeared behind the curtain. Safe for the moment. He lifted his head and turned once again to the arrogant young resident.

He nodded in the direction where Nicole had been. "What's going on in three?" he asked, and took a sip of the quickly cooling bitter shit in his cup. Forcing himself to swallow, he tried to act nonchalant. His throat burned with the acidic aftertaste, making him remember why he always stuck with soda.

"Hmm?"

Prick.

"Oh." The dickwad newbie waved it off as inconsequential. "A woman in labor. We're just waiting on L and D to come and get her."

He wanted to take the kid by the throat and squeeze until his eyes bulged. "Fine," he said instead. Nicole stepped back into the hall. "I've got to do a follow-up on a patient. You're in charge until I return." He backed away, making sure to keep one eye on Nicole.

"Dr. Emerson, there's a call for you on line one."

He whipped around at the petite voice behind him. One of the nurses. She smiled and batted her eyelashes.

"Take a message." He turned on his heel and hurried off. Slipping into a mostly unused stairwell, he stood where he could look out the tiny window and clearly see the ER. Nicole's back was to him now but every few seconds she glanced over her shoulder with a nervous twitch.

She scampered around the curtain once more right before a nurse he recognized from L and D arrived and followed her.

Stupid little cunt. What the hell was she doing here? His cock hardened. She was a cute thing. Be even cuter when he had his hands wrapped around her throat. The fabric of his green scrubs tented over his erection just like it had the other day and he reached down to stroke it. Coming down her throat while she struggled to breathe would stay with him for a long time. Now was not the fucking time though. He ripped his hand away from his weeping cock and slapped at the wall.

Minutes later, the trio of women exited the cubicle. A heavily pregnant woman gripped the wheelchair arms with tight fists. He smiled as she grimaced in pain and doubled over as much as her fat belly would allow.

"Hopefully it's a fucking boy," he sneered.

Nicole reached over and patted the woman's shoulder and then they were gone from sight.

"I've got you cornered, sweetheart. My hospital, my ER." He straightened the white lab coat and stethoscope around his neck before running his fingers through his hair.

He took a deep breath and stepped out of the stairwell to the familiar sounds of his space. Missy was the nurse on duty in triage and with a confident glide he strode into the small unit where patients were first monitored before being seen by a physician. Since she spread her legs for him whenever he wanted her to, he wasn't worried that she'd question him about what he was about to do. He'd have to take care of her soon though. There were only so many times he could fuck her before the impulse drove him to draw blood from her exquisite little body.

"Missy," he murmured, sliding his hand over her Snoopy and Woodstock covered ass.

"Dr. Emerson." Even the purring of her voice couldn't override the boner he sported over Nicole and the images of her in his mind.

He sat at the computer and pulled up a list of the latest patients seen by Missy. In times of heavy traffic, people were seen based on the severity of the injury. Fortunately today wasn't one of those times. They were fairly quiet so it wasn't hard to find out the name of prego.

He memorized the name then thumbed through the overhead cabinet, faking the need for a Band-Aid to throw Missy off track. Caressing his shoulder with the long fingernails of one hand, Missy smiled at him and reached over his head to grab the box.

"Let me get those for you, Alex." Her breasts rubbed against his upper arm and she licked her lips with the provocative tip of her tongue.

He loved the way she said his name. Alex turned into her and mouthed one of her hard-tipped nipples, leaving a wet ring on her turquoise shirt.

Fuck. He'd have her bent over the desk here in a minute. He stood with an abrupt motion, making Missy shriek in surprise.

"Later, angel," he breathed in her ear. She squirmed beneath his towering figure and winked as he walked away.

"Tieran Graham. Tieran Graham," Alex chanted under his breath. Paper-pushing would have to wait until he rid his ER of Nicole. He fisted his hands together, popping the knuckles of one hand, then the other.

Flinging the door to the stairs open, he jogged up three flights to a less-used wing of the hospital where he knew there was a vacant doctor's lounge. Alex shed his lab coat and hung it in one of the empty lockers there. Babies weren't born quickly so he had a little time. He stopped at the vending machines, fed them some change and gobbled down a package of stale crackers and a soda while he thought about the best way to proceed.

He would have liked to have more time to formulate a dramatic plan but didn't want her to disappear on him again. What if she didn't stay? What if someone came to relieve her so she could go back into hiding?

Damn. Alex crumpled the plastic wrapper and stuffed it in an empty trashcan next to the door. He didn't have time to track her and hunt her down. He'd have to do it here and now.

Taking the stairs two at a time, he launched himself to the fourth floor. A glance out the small window showed the immediate area was clear. He stepped into the corridor.

To his right, the elevators dinged their arrival. The doors opened with a swoosh and two people disembarked. A woman, who promptly turned left down the long hallway lined with private birthing rooms. And a man, who paused and looked both ways with his hands on his hips before his gaze fell on then flicked over Alex. For a second, his heart pounded. It was the bodyguard.

Son of an ever-loving bitch!

Chapter Sixteen

What a goddamn clusterfuck. Eli's incisors sharpened to deadly points, his finger joints popped and tried to shift. Again. He fisted his hands and shoved them in his pockets. He'd been fighting off his wolf for more than thirty minutes now. Ever since he'd received Nikki's message telling him where she and Tieran were headed. How many hospitals were in this area? Could he delude himself into thinking the man they were looking for wasn't at this one? Who the fuck was he kidding? The asshole had laid in wait, watched them until they'd left, then tried to kill Nikki. He was here. Somewhere.

Which meant he had to get his mate out of here now. Even though Derek provided a certain amount of protection, Eli couldn't help but think it would never be as much as Eli or Caelan with their extra abilities. And Caelan would be a little too preoccupied with Tieran to be of much assistance if something happened. Hell, the killer had gotten around having all three of them with her one time, he sure as shit could do it again.

The door to the room he'd been pointed to at the nurse's station stood open and he heard Nikki-Raine murmuring something. Her words and tone were soft, lyrical, and if he wasn't so damn mad, scared—fuck was he scared—he might enjoy listening to it instead of her normal stubborn-ass mouth.

"I'll kill him, Nikki, I swear. He's a dead man. You're a dead man, do you hear me, Caelan?" Tieran's pained voice wobbled as she screamed.

Eli almost laughed. Almost. Then he remembered the reason he was standing here in the first place.

He stepped just inside the doorway, his heart slowing at the sight of his mate. Nikki was safe. For the moment. When he got his hands on her later tonight, he couldn't promise anything. A low growl reverberated in his chest and both women jerked their gazes his way.

Shit. Eli spread his feet apart and lifted his arms in the air. Nikki-Raine catapulted herself into them, wrapping her legs around his hips and bear hugging him with everything she had.

The action melted his anger a tiny fraction. He kissed her cheek, her eyebrows, her lips. Anything to taste her, make sure she really was still with him and not dead or kidnapped by some sadistic bastard. She shifted in his arms, letting him take all of her weight, and grasped his face with her hands. Her mouth met his in a hungry kiss, melding their tongues together.

If she thought to distract him, she was doing a damn fine job of it.

Eli wrestled his face away from her. Ha. Her chest heaved against his, which would have been good except his did the same against hers. She knew how to push every button in the book, the little snot. Holding onto her with one arm, he used the other to push her head out of the way so he could peer over her shoulder at his sister-in-law.

"You okay, Tieran?" Besides the fact she had hair matted all over her forehead and was sweating bullets.

"Mmm. 'S getting better." Tieran pinched her lips together and winced. Her hand reached for her belly and clutched at the blue flowered gown that barely covered her. At some point she'd kicked off the covers. Her toes curled with her obvious pain and Eli's head swam. He remembered exactly what it felt like to be in so much pain. Well, not that kind of pain, but the intensity for sure.

Shaking off the feeling and the memories of his time handcuffed to a hospital bed, he glanced around the room. When he didn't immediately see Derek, a low growl reverberated through his chest.

"Where is he?"

"Who?" Nikki asked, a questioning look on her face.

"What do you mean, who?" Eli couldn't help but shout.

"Shh," she hissed. "I thought he was with you."

"I swear to God, Nikki-Raine, you're pushing your luck."

She slapped him on the chest. "I'm not pushing anything. You were with Caelan, why didn't you bring him?"

He contained the urge to strangle her, barely. Only the fact she clearly looked confused kept him from wrapping his hands around her throat. "I'm not talking about him, Nik, he's on his way. I'm talking about Derek, who you said over the phone you would call. I don't see him, where is he?"

A strong wave of unsettled fear emanated off his mate and wafted across his nose. Good. She damn well needed to be scared. He wasn't about to be the only one.

"Umm, he's not here yet." She slowly untangled herself from his body and dropped to the floor.

"What did you say?" Eli couldn't keep the snarl out of his voice.

Nikki-Raine cleared her throat. "I said, he's not here, Eli. What the hell did you want us to do? Wait for him? Tieran's having a baby as you can clearly see."

Patience did not show itself. Not with the information Morales had given him. It didn't matter she hadn't been told yet. He took a semi-calming breath to clear his head. "There are things you don't know yet, Nikki." He grabbed both her shoulders, knowing he might very well tear her apart when she was just starting to feel safe.

"What things?" she asked, squinting in confusion.

Fuck. He hated this feeling of helplessness. Until they knew more about who they were looking for, he was helpless.

"Not here. We need to get out of here first."

"Eli," she hissed. "Your sister-in-law is about to have a baby. We can't just leave her here alone."

"Watch me." He grabbed her hand and started to drag her.

She resisted, making him turn back to her. He wanted to howl, to show everyone in this godforsaken hospital how pissed he was.

Nikki bit her lip. Her anxious eyes darted every which way but at him. "Tell me what things you're talking about."

"Damn it, you are one stubborn woman." He too glanced around, but saw no one.

"Morales called. They let the boyfriend go."

She gasped and sank her fingernails into his forearms. Her face drained of all color. "No," she whispered.

"Yes. And they've found the leak in their department."

She shook her head wildly. Eli drew her into a hug.

"They're trying to find out where the killer called him from," he murmured, rubbing a hand up and down her back and kissing the top of her head.

"Oh, God." Her forehead rolled back and forth on his chest and her shoulders tensed beneath his hands. "There's something I need to tell you."

Why did she sound so ominous? His body rumbled in response. "What?" Damn. He rubbed a hand over his face. Yelling at her wasn't doing anyone a bit of good.

Nikki yanked her head back in shock. "Stop growling, you ass, before you disturb Tieran." She grabbed his arm this time and pulled him further into the hall.

"I'm sorry," he murmured when they stopped. He brought her fingers to his mouth and rubbed his lips across her shaky knuckles. Her pulse hammered at her wrist and he could smell the urgent stench of fear. Leaning back, Eli turned her face up to his with a finger beneath her chin and searched her eyes. Something had happened. "What's wrong?"

Nikki pulled out of his grasp and twisted her fingers together in front of her belly. "I...nothing," she said, dropping her chin to her chest.

Warning bells clanged in his head. "Nikki-Raine."

She shrugged, infuriating him with her casualness.

"I don't know. When we first got here I...got an uneasy feeling, that's all. Maybe just from being here too many times with the accident and then the shooting. And then the other shooting. I tried not to think about it too much since he'd been caught, but..." Nikki trailed off.

Eli finished her line of thinking. But now they knew the real killer was still out there.

She shivered and he brought her close again. If she'd felt strange about something, he believed her. Shifters used their sixth senses all the time, why shouldn't she?

"Oops, sorry."

Eli turned at the sound of his brother barreling down the hallway and nearly taking out a nurse. His twin righted the poor woman without slowing down and almost toppled him and

Nikki. Eli couldn't contain his laugh, dispelling the tense situation, and steadied the red-faced father-to-be.

"A little anxious there, Cael?"

"More than you know," Caelan huffed, pale-faced and breathless. He pounded Eli on the back.

Caelan turned and grasped Nikki's shoulders, then leaned in to kiss her soundly on the cheek. "Thank you for bringing her in."

Eli growled. "You've got a mate already."

Caelan, the bastard, paid no attention to Eli again. Who did he think he was? Prime or no Prime, twin or not, Caelan didn't need to be touching *his* mate. "Go touch your own woman," Eli snarled, tucking Nikki-Raine more firmly into his side.

Again, no response. From either one of them.

"Thank you for putting your life in danger to help me. Tieran, I mean. You'll never know how much that means to me." His eyes glittered even in the not-so-great lights of the hallway.

"You just told me," Nikki-Raine replied sweetly.

Where the hell was that tone when she spoke to him?

"Besides, I didn't have much choice. Birthing babies isn't my thing," she muttered, turning to glare at Eli.

"No you didn't have a choice," Caelan said. "But we'll talk about that later. And since I figure Eli's already filled you in on the killer, you two need to get out of here."

"We will," Eli replied. "Keep an eye on your own backs, huh?"

Caelan nodded. "I've got a couple of the guys coming out just in case. I have a feeling I won't be able to do much."

Caelan turned and marched proudly into the room. But not before Eli witnessed the green tinge to his skin.

"Let's go," Eli growled, taking her elbow and pushing her toward the elevators.

"Wait."

Eli's arm was jerked almost out of his socket when she stopped abruptly. Because he hadn't let go of her arm he was jerked around to face her. He didn't like the look on her face.

Chapter Seventeen

Eli lifted her face to his with the crook of his finger. "What's going on, Nikki?" His thumb rubbed lazily along her bottom lip, making her tummy quiver. Her nostrils flared. They were in the middle of a crisis and she wanted him.

Payback could be a bitch. Maybe she could even use it to her advantage because right now, anything that took his mind off questioning her was a good thing. She didn't want to talk about how she'd felt down in that ER earlier. Especially not in light of the fact this Josh wasn't who the police thought he was. So what had she seen when they'd first gotten here?

Nikki tried to smile. Tried to make him think nothing was wrong by giving him a wicked look. Eli grunted.

"Fuck. Stop looking at me like that," he groaned, and shifted his stance to adjust himself in his jeans.

Who was she kidding? She couldn't seduce. Not now anyway. It was a nervous reaction in a tense situation.

"Hey," he said, stroking his thumb over her cheek. His mouth descended on hers, lips caressing, soft. Sensitive.

For a second anyway. He angled her head and sealed their lips, drinking from her like a dehydrated man on his fifth day in the desert with no water.

No matter how wrong this was, she couldn't help the moan that slipped out, or the way her hands lifted to his chest. The T-shirt stood in her way, keeping her from what she really wanted—the taut muscles of his bare chest. She loved the feel of his skin under hers, loved to feel him jump whenever she touched a particularly sensitive spot.

Eli jerked back and stood on unsteady feet. He wiped his mouth with the back of his hand, then wiggled a finger at her.

"You little witch. You're trying to distract me."

What the hell? She hadn't done a damn thing. Okay, she had, but he didn't need to know that. "Excuse me, but *you* attacked *me*."

He snorted. "Attacked? I hardly think kissing you is attacking you, and you wanted it."

"You wanted it," Nikki mocked, turning the tables on him.

"I'll always fucking want you."

Nikki sighed. Back to the growling yet again. "That's not my problem."

Except it was, because she wanted him just as much as he wanted her. That stupid mate-link thing, she guessed.

"Talk."

"Ugh. When we first got here, we were in the ER and had to wait for someone to come and get Tieran. I got this...tingly feeling and the hair stood up on the back of my neck. But when I looked around, I didn't see anybody other than two doctors."

Eli nodded and waved at her to continue when she paused.

"That's all. It happened again when they walked by, but when they passed, so did the feeling."

The strangest look came over his face. Did his face seem paler? What was going on?

"Did you recognize either of them?" he asked.

Nikki shrugged. "The one never lifted his head up. He had dark hair, but..." She ground the heels of her hands into her eye sockets and sucked in a breath. "God. I don't know. The other one was only about twenty."

"So you think a twenty-year-old can't do the sort of things you saw."

She shook her head. "How the hell should I know?"

Eli sighed. "It doesn't matter. Maybe your subconscious recognized him somehow. All the more reason for us to get the hell out of here." He reached for her hand, ready to pull her along after him.

She resisted again, shaking her head. "I can't, Eli."

"What the hell do you mean, you can't?" His eyelids lowered into menacing slits.

"What if this is my chance to find out who killed my friends?"

"This is insane," he barked. "No way."

"Please," she begged softly.

Eli stomped his foot and threaded his fingers through his hair. "It's too dangerous."

"You're here, we're in a crowded hospital. We can stand back out of the way and watch." She laid a hand on his arm. "Please."

He threw his head back. For a second there, she thought he might howl. She wasn't too far off. When he looked at her again, his eyes glowed. His lip curled back, revealing lengthened, razor-sharp canines. Nikki sucked in a breath. She'd seen him in wolf form but never this...in-between form. His body twitched as if he were trying to contain the wolf inside him.

"I need to do this, Eli." She wrapped her arms around his middle and hugged him to her. His chest vibrated with a low growl.

He sighed and returned her embrace, nuzzling his chin on the top of her head. "You think you can pick the same guys out again?"

Nikki's heart thumped. She moved her hands lower and fisted his shirt. Her fingertips brushed something hard at the small of his back. His hand met hers and lifted them higher.

"My gun, sweetheart," he said in her ear so no one would hear him.

She nodded. She knew he carried one.

"You didn't answer my question."

"I honestly don't know, Eli. I only saw the top of his head. If you want a description it was dark brown and round. So was the killer's. So is half the population's."

"Fine. Let's get this over with and go home."

"Thank you. I know you don't want to." She glanced up at him, knowing there were unshed tears in her eyes.

"You're right. I think I should get you out of here. I don't want anyone taking another potshot at you. But I can also see how much you want to do this."

She could have corrected him. Should have. There was no *want* involved here. She *needed* to do this. For Lou and Kelly and Amy.

Eli tugged her down the hallway and stood waiting at the elevator with his hand on the small of her back. His gaze constantly searched the area.

The elevator doors opened with a ding and Eli pushed Nikki-Raine inside. The compartment was empty. Once the doors shut with a swoosh, he guided her to a side wall. With one hand holding her firmly in place, he reached out to the control panel and pressed the Lobby button. As the car began its descent, Eli skimmed Nikki's cheekbone with his thumb in a tender caress. He pressed his forehead to hers, closed his eyes and sighed. He would never get enough of her smell. So sweet, so sexy.

So why in the hell was he letting her do this?

Leaning closer, he murmured against her lips. "God, I love you." Her body dissolved with the slightest of kisses. "I don't know what I would have done if something had happened to you today. Promise me you won't take a chance like this again," he growled, barely containing his canines from lengthening.

And I promise never to let you get into this kind of situation again.

"Have any more pregnant women on the ranch you plan on leaving helpless?" she teased, reaching up and lacing her fingers together at the back of his neck.

His cock leapt to attention. Didn't matter they were in a seriously ugly situation, he wanted her.

"No." Eli took control of her mouth in a possessive kiss. He swept his tongue past her lips, tasting and consuming her until everything else faded away.

She broke the kiss, coming up for air and breathing as heavily as he was. "What were we talking about?"

"You, never leaving the ranch again." He squeezed her in a tight hug until she squeaked. Bending for another kiss, he barely comprehended the lurch of the car when it came to a stop at the lobby. The bell dinged and the doors opened. Passengers piled in. They had to fight their way off through the crowd.

Once outside he whipped around, keeping Nikki-Raine pressed between him and the wall. His mate's life had been threatened enough. This would end here, today.

Knowing she was as scared as him, Eli reached back and took hold of her hand. It trembled in his. If he could kick his own ass, he would. He shouldn't be allowing this. He should throw her over his shoulder and storm out to the car where he could drive her away from all this. Except they'd still be trapped in this mess. He yanked his cell phone from his belt clip and called the detective. He needed to know what they were about to do. He felt her rest her forehead between his shoulder blades and heard a small sigh. Her fingers alternately opened and closed on his back. Morales' voice mail picked up and Eli left a message telling him the circumstances and where they were.

In a few minutes this would all be over and he could take her home. To bed where he could make love to her until she forgot about being scared if even for an hour.

Nikki held her breath. Her stomach tightened into knots. Sweat trickled down her back and gathered on her upper lip. Her palm felt slimy against his shirt.

He must have sensed her stress because he turned to face her. Rubbing both her arms up and down helped ward off the sudden chill and goose bumps overtaking the sweat.

"Damn, Nik. If you don't want to do this, we don't have to." His thumb lifted her chin until she looked into his eyes. "Did you hear me?"

She hesitated. They did have to do it. She didn't want to live in fear anymore. It was time to take back her life. To face her future. One complete with a hairy shape-shifting werewolf and his wacky family. She inhaled deeply and nodded.

"Is that a yes for you don't want to do this, or a yes, you do?"

"I do," she whispered.

Screw this. What would being a pansy-assed little girl get her? Nothing but more time at the ranch jail. Nikki threw her shoulders back and held her chin high. "I do."

"That's my girl." Eli's ragged smile was insincere, she knew. *He* clearly didn't want to do this. Eli placed a sweet kiss on her lips and mustered the determination to drag her through the ER.

The amount of activity had greatly increased since they'd first arrived. Several of the curtained areas had patients, and nurses and doctors were swarming the space.

How in the hell was she supposed to spot the brown-haired, round-headed someone in all this commotion? "There's too many people here, Eli. Too many brown heads," she said, pulling on his hand. Her heart pounded. The air seemed too thin. Dizziness threatened to take over and her knees wobbled.

"Try, Nikki-Raine, that's all we can do for now. I want to catch this guy so we can get on with our lives without having to look over our shoulders. Besides, we aren't counting on your recognition of his hair color, we're acting on your gut feelings." He kissed her again.

The smooth, soft touch settled her nerves.

"I'm not Tieran, E. I don't have psychic abilities."

"Thank God." He laughed. "I couldn't handle it if you were." Eli gave a mock shiver. "It's kind of scary what she can do."

"And turning into a wolf isn't scary at all?"

"Yeah, but—"

"But nothing, E. It's over-the-top creepy."

Eli growled low in his throat. Nikki smiled. She loved riling him. The truth of the matter was he didn't scare her in his wolf form. He gave her a little push at the small of her back and they moved again.

A flourish of activity near the ambulance bay doors distracted them. A team of doctors and nurses approached from behind just as the double doors sprung apart. Paramedics pushed through and suddenly Eli and Nikki were sucked into the pack of converging personnel. Police officers and firefighters filed in also, adding to the confusion.

Feeling crushed, Nikki panicked. She was forced to let go of Eli's hand or have her arm ripped off. Another ambulance arrived and with it, more people. The sound of shouting doctors and stomping feet along with the regular cacophony of an excited crowd made her ears ring.

"Eli," she shouted, standing on her tiptoes to try and locate him. She stumbled when someone bumped into her, pushing her into an IV stand. Her ankle twisted sharply. She yelped as it gave out, making her fall to the ground. "Shit." Nikki pressed her lips together and tried to hold back the burn of tears in her eyes. Her ankle throbbed. A shoe came dangerously close to stepping on the fingers she had outstretched on the floor for support.

Looking up did no good. There were too many people. Damn. "Eli," she yelled again. No one even looked in her direction. Why would they look at a person sitting on the floor in a hospital? Did they think this was the only spot she could find to sit? If she stayed here long enough, Eli would eventually make his way back to her. She shivered at the thought.

When the mass finally thinned a bit, she attempted to stand. Her ankle protested with an angry flare of pain shooting up her leg. A hard arm clamped around her waist and drew her up into a steely chest. She sighed and relaxed into it, feeling the vibration of his chest against her back.

"'Bout time," she sighed. How long had she been sitting there? Surely just a couple of minutes. Her heart's pounding slowly started to fade into a more normal rhythm. She allowed herself to be pulled...dragged, more like it, away from the throng. In moments she found herself in a dark space looking out into the bright hallway.

"I didn't think we were ever going to get out of that," she breathed, reaching for a light switch on the wall. The door swung shut, blocking out every speck of light, leaving her blind. Sucking in a sharp breath, Nikki blinked, trying to adjust to the blackness.

Something brushed her shoulder and she heard the distinct click of a lock being thrown into place.

Her senses went into hyper-alert. Every smell and sound intensified. Every smell...oh, Jesus. Nikki threw herself against the door but before she could raise her arm to bang on it, her wrist was caught in a punishing grip and a sweaty palm covered her mouth. She barely had enough space to breathe through her nose.

Chapter Eighteen

"It was so nice of you to come to me." The stench of sour coffee washed over her. "And to think, I'd been led to believe I'd already gotten rid of you." The fingertips of his free hand slid over her cheek and across the bridge of her nose, only to return to tangle in her hair. She gagged behind his hand, her eyes tearing.

Nikki squirmed in the bruising hold he had around her neck, prying at his hand with her fingers until he subdued her. He yanked her arms to her sides and crushed her to his chest. She whimpered. Her nose ran, making breathing even more difficult.

"Where have you been hiding, my pretty?" He chuckled, his body swaying with hers as if he were dancing. Her feet shuffled on the floor. "The cops actually pulled one over on me. Hats off to them. It won't happen again." His voice feathered along her ear in an eerie whisper.

"Still got the bodyguard, huh?" he asked, his voice rising. "Don't leave home without him?" He laughed as if he'd made a joke.

Nikki's heart slammed inside her so hard it hurt. Her nostrils flared with each attempt to draw air, and still the whimper sounded. She squeezed her eyes closed and prayed the door would burst open and Eli would storm in. He could smell her, right? He'd find her soon.

But would it be soon enough?

The man laid his cheek on her head and hummed, still swaying, and clutched her tighter. His erect penis ground into the small of her back. Something in her snapped. Tieran's vision popped into her head. This was it. The dark room, the fear.

She would not be a victim again.

Nikki scrambled to think. To forget about everything except Eli and getting the hell out of here.

What should she do? Play the innocent? Keep him talking? Give Eli time to find her. She could do this.

"Wha new oo wan?"

"You make any move to scream and I'll slit your throat before it ever comes out, understand?"

She nodded once.

"What were you saying?" He released her mouth just enough so she could speak, but ready to cover it immediately after.

"What do you want?" Nikki caught her breath. "Who are you?" Please God let this work.

"Don't play dumb with me, bitch. You know exactly who I am." His angry hiss reverberated through the dark. "You aren't going to ruin my game. If I had known you were still alive, I'd have done something sooner, had a nice scenario planned. Now I have to wing it." He grasped her neck with bruising fingers and Nikki flinched.

How much time had gone by? They weren't that far away. Where was Eli? *Please, hurry, E.* The man moved behind her.

"I don't know what you're talking about. I'm here with a friend who's pregnant." Talk about winging it. Her eyes had adjusted now. A strip of light seeped under the door. Nikki turned her head at the rustle of clothes. He was standing to her side now. Still too close. "Please, I haven't been hiding," she pleaded, hoping to sound convincing. Damn, playing dumb was harder than she thought. "I have a bodyguard because of my ex, that's all. I swear."

I love you, Eli.

"You don't have a bodyguard anymore," he sneered. "Don't expect him to come to your rescue."

Nikki's knees almost buckled. God, no. No. She'd know in her heart if he was gone. He had to be lying to her. *Please, God, let him be lying to me.* The air shifted in front of her and she automatically reached out to fend him off. He grabbed her hands in midair, the action making her think of Eli and his unnatural ability to see in the dark. Was this man one of them? Could he shift too?

Screw the innocent act. She wasn't going to make it out of here alive. He forced her hands behind her back, binding them together somehow and Nikki inhaled to scream. A staggering punch to her belly sucked all the air out of her lungs. Her stomach revolted, sending vomit into her throat, and her knees collapsed.

He caught her when she would have fallen to the ground, by yanking on the arms tied behind her. Her shoulders screamed in agony and this time a loud shriek erupted from her lips. He backhanded her, splitting her lip. The tangy, metallic taste of blood flooded her mouth. A second later he slammed her against the wall. Pain exploded at the back of her head, and stars danced in front of her.

"Fucking cunt," he spat. "Don't fucking make a sound or I'll kill you now."

He would kill her anyway, she thought wildly. Why did the when matter?

His taunting voice filled the room. "What does it feel like to get shot, hmm? I've always wondered." His breath was hot on her already sweating face.

Nikki gulped several times trying to regain her equilibrium. She bit savagely on the freshly cut lip, desperate for anything to keep her focused, and forced back tears of pain.

"I want you to fucking admit you saw something you shouldn't have and that you know who I am. It will make killing you that much more gratifying." His hand shot to her face and squeezed her chin. "Did you like what you saw?"

Nikki sobbed and fought to get better footing. She was up against something and her feet couldn't find a proper spot. "I don't know what you're talking about," she cried. She would rip him to shreds. Jesus, just remembering Lou and her friends made her want to puke.

"Was she a good friend of yours? She tried to fight me tooth and nail while I fucked her." He laughed. "I like a woman who fights, but in the end, she was no match for me." His tongue swept a path up her cheek. Breathing hard now, Nikki jerked her head away.

She stopped squirming. If he wanted a fight, he wouldn't get one from her.

"She was nice and tight. Perfect, really. Are you tight, or has your bodyguard lover ruined you for me?"

He cupped her through her jeans with one hand and cut off her scream with the other.

"You bastard." Her shout came out muffled. She brought her knee up with the intent to dislodge him and felt the slightest of pricks against her neck. The pressure increased until she realized he held the razor edge of something sharp on her throat.

"There, there. I knew you'd remember," he cooed, continuing to fondle her crotch. "I promise to make it good for you." His tongue darted out and swiped her ear.

Nikki gagged on the bile rushing to the surface again. She tightened her legs together around his hand, and he pressed her into the wall, cutting off her air supply.

"Do not make a sound, or I'll slit your throat."

The knife moved away only to be replaced by his fingers in a furious grip around her windpipe, but at least he'd relinquished his hold between her legs.

He was going to rape her. Nikki's stomach turned over and that day in the mall parking lot flashed through her mind. She'd gotten away from them, she could get away from him. If only she were telepathic. *Eli.*

A small pull on her shirt distracted her. He cut the thick cotton with the extremely sharp blade as if it were the finest of silks. The shirt parted and fell to the sides, revealing her bra-clad breasts, and a puff of cool air washed across her tummy. Goose bumps prickled her skin from head to toe.

His fingertips caressed her, trailing down from the hollow at her throat to the button on her jeans. The man laughed when her stomach muscles jerked in terror. A whimper of hate and protest burst from her lips.

"Ah, ah, ah. I told you, no sounds." He admonished her almost playfully. His fingers continued wandering, stopping at the front clasp of her bra.

With her arms pinned behind her she couldn't stop him. A quick flick of his wrist and her small breasts fell free from their confinement.

"I wish I could see what color your nipples are." He plucked them in a tight pinch.

Nikki threw her head side to side. His pinch grew unbearable until she stopped.

"They're budding. You can't control their response. It's natural."

He stood there, raping her, yet talking as if he were her lover. Her mind faded in and out, everything she'd learned leaving as quickly as it formed. She wanted to thrust her knee up into his groin and smash his dick into smithereens. Her feet felt weighed down by concrete blocks. Without her hands, she didn't have many more options.

His hand crushed her windpipe until spots swam in her dark vision. His whispered spoutings became background noise.

In her waning strength, she felt the pressure at her waist released with the rasp of her zipper. His hands fumbled between them as she struggled to get out of his hold. Her body grew numb from the lack of oxygen.

Never seeing Eli again was a fate far worse than being raped and killed.

Eli groaned. The floor was cold and hard beneath his cheek. A burning sensation tore through a spot on his neck and he fumbled to wipe his fingertips across the ache. His arms felt weighed down with lead. Where the fuck was he? Peeling his eyelids open was hell but he knew there was something he was supposed to be doing.

Damn it, what had happened?

Ever so slowly his senses started firing. He'd been in the car and gotten a call from Morales. Eli blinked in the darkness. Only a tiny sliver of light protruded the black surroundings. It took a few minutes for his wolf's eyesight to kick in. When it did, he was more confused than before.

Wooden shelves graced both sides of the narrow space he lay in. Some were shielded with glass, some open. A few spaces were locked with a keypad. Folded white bundles were stacked on one shelf from floor to ceiling.

Eli groaned again and ran his hands over his face.

"Son of a bitch," he bit out. What the hell was going on? "Think, Eli, think." He closed his eyes and inhaled, relying on his wolf to sense his surroundings. The strong smell of antiseptic filled his nostrils. He froze, fingers dug into his eye sockets.

One minute he'd been escorting Nikki through the ER, the next they'd been separated. He remembered a sharp poke in his neck and then nothing. His heart pounded in revelation and before he knew it, he'd shifted. Eli snarled at the thick door holding him in the tiny closet. Whoever was on the other side was about to get a show.

He backed up as far as the opposite wall would allow and with a howl charged the door. Some speck of sanity must have remained because at the last second, he shifted and slammed into the door. The wood splintered off the doorframe and flew outward. Several screams rent the air. Eli ignored the gasps and strange looks, rolled to his feet and scented the air.

He had to fight to keep his wolf at bay. How many long minutes had they been separated? How long had he been out cold? A quick glance at his watch showed only about fifteen minutes had passed since they'd walked off the elevator. He remembered looking at the time then. Fifteen minutes. They could be fucking anywhere.

Tuning out the chaos around him, Eli fisted his hands almost unconsciously. His heart thumped in an erratic pattern. Every joint in his body itched to shift, and his skin crawled with the impending change. In a minute he wouldn't be able to help himself.

Lungs heaving, he plastered himself to the wall. His nostrils flared with every inhalation. Closing his eyes, Eli focused his senses. Nikki had to still be here. He wouldn't accept anything else. Drawing on every ounce of his abilities to hunt as the wolf, he searched for her.

The room around him grew silent, the noise faded to the background until there was nothing but himself and his mate's fading scent. To his right, which meant she hadn't gone outside since the door was to his left. Another acrid scent mingled with hers. It smelled of anger and fear. Of course it could belong to any number of the people in the ER, but somehow it seemed to be wrapped around Nikki's.

More composed, Eli pushed off the wall. He lifted his nose in the air and followed the trail. He nearly bumped into Caelan as he rounded a corner.

"Eli, what the hell are you doing? Where's Nikki?"

"She's gone. We got separated. He took her." Jesus, he couldn't even form a complete thought. He covered the spot on his neck where the prick had apparently injected him with something. Probably something meant to knock a grown man out for a long time. Bastard didn't know how quickly a wolf healed, even when drugged.

"What?" he snarled. "What the fuck happened?"

Eli grabbed Caelan's forearms, drawing on the strength of the Prime. "Nikki said she saw someone down here who made

202

her feel weird when she first got here with Tieran..." It suddenly dawned on him. "Where is Tieran?"

"In her room, with our son. I called your cell and got your voice mail a minute ago. Tieran needed something I have in my car, so that's where I was heading."

"Fuck. Nikki wanted to try and find the bastard again, but the ER got swarmed. She was ripped right out of my hands." He held them up and stared at them.

Caelan inspected the area where Eli had fingered his throat. "The fucker shot you up with something," he growled. His thumb traced the small needle mark and his eyes glowed with barely contained menace. In a minute they'd both be in trouble. All these people would get a good idea of who—what— really lived among them.

Caelan grabbed Eli's elbow and moved them in the direction Eli had been heading. "Keep talking," he barked.

"It was goddamn fast. By the time I turned around she was gone. He'll kill her," he whispered.

Caelan leaned in close to Eli, detecting Nikki's scent on him and together they picked up the trail. It ended at a different, locked supply closet. Eli laid his hand on the door. She was definitely in there. Still alive.

He drew a breath he hadn't realized he was holding.

"This is what Tieran meant before, a dark place... Motherfucker. She's in there with him." Eli hissed. His ears picked up almost every minute sound.

Eli stood shoulder-to-shoulder with Caelan, ready to bust through the thick, solid wood door. Together each of them lashed out with a foot. The frame splintered and the door flew inward, slamming into the wall inside.

Light flooded the dark storage room. Inside a man turned sharply, eyes wide and glistening in the spill of light like an animal caught in a car's headlights. The sudden illumination must have blinded him because he rubbed at his eyes. He groped behind his back and dragged Nikki-Raine's limp form to his front and held her to his chest with a choking arm around her neck. Her head fell forward.

Eli's heart sank. They were too late. She was gone. A keening sound filled the room and he felt as though his knees would collapse. He lifted the gun he had no recollection of drawing and aimed it at the bastard's forehead.

"He's got a knife." Caelan's hand rested on his shoulder, giving it a slight squeeze.

Eli zeroed in on what Caelan saw. The doctor, still in his scrubs, crushed Nikki to him with his left hand and held the edge of a scalpel just below her ear with his right. Eli's heart threatened to burst. He clamped his jaw tight and his chest vibrated with a low, fierce growl.

Nikki's T-shirt hung loosely open, revealing angry red bruises already forming on her breasts. Her jeans were unzipped and pushed down around her hips to the point where the curly hair between her legs peeked out over the rumpled lace of her underwear.

At least he hadn't been able to fucking rape her. Her fingers twitched, drawing his attention. Alive.

Eli shook his head. His mate needed him now. Needed him sane to get her out of this, not giving in to the rage simmering in his veins.

Time slowed. Beside him, Caelan raised his own gun, beading in on the same spot Eli had no doubt. There was no more movement, no sound but the harshness of all their breathing.

A wisp of air near his ear told him someone else had entered the room. Eli didn't look. He kept his entire being centered on the scumbag who held his heart in filthy hands.

He and the doctor stared at each other. The killer smiled and broke the tension first.

"Well, well. It's seems you've caught me." He stroked Nikki's cheek with his thumb, leaving the blade pressed against what Eli knew to be the velvet soft skin of her neck. Keeping his eyes trained on Eli, the bastard bent his head and licked the path his thumb had wandered. "Too bad she didn't live long enough for me to have some fun. So tasty." He laughed.

Eli saw red.

"You'll never get out of here," he spat.

"No, it doesn't seem likely, does it? Too bad it has to end because some bitch saw me." His arms tightened around her flimsy body.

"Let. Her. Go." An eerie calmness took over, keeping Eli from leaping at the man. Only knowing he might hurt Nikki worse than she was prevented him from doing so. She was no more dead than he was.

"I can't do that."

"Why not? If she's dead, she's no bargaining chip to you anymore." Damn it hurt to say those words. "Let her go and end this peacefully." Eli took a step forward. There wouldn't be any peace in this room.

"Don't come any closer or I'll slit her throat."

Eli had to take a gamble. "I thought you said she was dead?" He swallowed before speaking again and sent up a prayer that Nikki couldn't hear him. "You're going to slit her throat anyway, aren't you? You don't want to be the only one leaving here in a body bag." His hands shook. "You want her to be your last hurrah." He took another step.

"Stop." The man's hand tightened on the scalpel.

Eli caught the metallic stench of blood and even in the gloomy confines could see the drop of Nikki's blood well up on the edge of the scalpel. He jerked to a standstill, freezing in his spot.

Inhaling deeply, he hoped he hadn't pushed too hard, and made a serious error in judgement.

"Let's make a deal. You don't kill her, I won't kill you?"

The man laughed again, the sound grating on every one of Eli's nerves. His wolf howled silently, begging to be let loose. It was harder than anything he'd ever done not to shift and rip out the bastard's throat. But to do that would be a death sentence on his people. Too many would witness his change and condemn him to a life of scientists and possibly ferret out the rest of the pack. He wouldn't let that happen.

"Death is better than prison any day. Life is like a prison, isn't it? You say I'm a murderer, I say I've released all these souls from their prisons." His thumb caressed her cheek again.

He was relaxing. Stupid fool. Keep him talking, get him off-kilter and go in for the kill.

"Wouldn't you want her to have better than her prison of a life?" he continued.

Fucking demented bastard. Less than five feet separated them. Eli could take him out, but with how much risk to Nikki?

"I saw you with her earlier. You had your tongue down her throat."

Nikki moaned.

"Is she a good fuck?"

With an animalistic growl and superhuman speed, Eli lunged at him. A girlish scream erupted from Nikki's attacker who'd been unprepared for the assault. He reacted instinctively, just as Eli hoped he would, dropping his hold on Nikki to defend himself.

Nikki slumped to the floor with a soft whimper. In their scuffle, Eli's foot connected with something soft and he cringed. They came together, arms raised, grunting with the force of the impact.

Eli felt the cold steel of the knife slice through his forearm, but didn't release his hold. They stayed upright, the killer trying to stab Eli, and Eli trying to club him with his gun.

Caelan yelled. "Get down, E."

Several other shouts of "freeze" or "don't move" penetrated Eli's one-track mind.

Out of his peripheral vision, Eli saw someone move closer and drag Nikki to safety. With her body out of the way, the two men found themselves falling in the freed space, like a wall had disappeared.

Eli tried to gain the upper hand by twisting in midair so the other man would be beneath him. It didn't work. They landed hard on the ground, Eli on his right side, with a whoosh of air and a groan of pain, neither one of them surrendering their hold.

Eli's head hit the concrete with a sickening thud, making him see stars for a split second. The killer took advantage, thrusting his blade upward.

The knife plunged into Eli's abdomen with a tight, hot pinch. Someone yelled. Eli fought to bring his gun hand up from underneath the bastard's body, but it was pinned to the floor.

Warmth flooded his belly along with a burn that wouldn't quit.

Eli heard a volley of shits, and fucks and get-out-of-the-ways. There wasn't enough room for many other people and certainly not enough to get a shot off.

His right temple throbbed, threatening to cut off his grip on the world. He lifted his head in time to see Caelan charging closer. The killer raised his arm, anchoring his body off the floor with his left elbow and giving Eli the chance he needed.

Eli twisted his wrist and squeezed his finger. His ears rang. The man's body collapsed over him, heavy against Eli's battered body. The last thing he saw was Caelan standing over them, looking grim.

Chapter Nineteen

Grogginess cluttered Eli's mind and he couldn't for the life of him figure out why. Pain wracked every inch of his body. The last time he'd felt like this, he'd been face down on the concrete being accused of killing... Fuuuucckk.

He inhaled and started to stretch his aching muscles, but stopped short when the strong smell of antiseptic abraded his nostrils. Where in the hell was he? Eli lifted one eyelid to inspect his surroundings, wincing when the dull light from above shot arrows through his brain.

When the pain dissipated, he tried again. Must be a hell of a hangover. He reached for Nikki, seeking her warm, soft skin, but his arm refused to obey.

Oh hell, not again. If he was handcuffed to a fucking bed again—

"Hey, glad to see you're back amongst the living."

Caelan? In his bedroom?

No. Not his bedroom. They'd been at the hospital and Nikki had been in the arms of that bastard. He lunged upward, instantly grabbing his side when a knifelike pain radiated through his abs. Eli toppled over onto his back again then rolled and tried to bring his knees up. The movement made the pain worse.

"Take it easy." Caelan's hand landed on his shoulder and aided him in turning back over.

"Where is she?" Eli gasped. "Where's Nikki-Raine?" He didn't care about the pain anymore, only getting to his mate. He struggled to sit up and again Caelan forced him down.

"She's asleep, moron, and you'll wake her up if you don't control yourself."

Eli's eyes widened. He twisted to see her. She was lying on her side in another bed, facing him, her knees pulled up to her chest, one hand tucked beneath her cheek, the other on the pillow beside her. An ugly bruise stretched across her cheekbone.

"How is she?" he whispered, wanting more than anything to get up and go to her, shield her from life itself.

"She's fine. Better than you anyway. A few bruises on her throat, the one on her face. Doc said her larynx wasn't crushed, just bruised."

"What the fuck are you talking about?" he snapped, his gaze tracking the skin he could see.

"He tried to choke her, E. Her throat will be sore for a few days, but other than that, she'll be fine."

Eli reached an arm toward her, ignoring the fire pulling at his side.

Who cared if he woke her up? He had to hear her voice, to know for himself she was okay.

"Nikki-Raine, I'm here, baby."

She didn't move and Eli felt a stab of worry.

"Why won't she wake up?" he growled.

Caelan snorted. "Doc had to give her a mild sedative to help her sleep. After she woke up from passing out earlier, she wouldn't let anyone look at her because she didn't know how you were. When we'd finally convinced her you were going to be okay, she relented. But only after she demanded to be in the same room as you." He shuffled his feet and muttered, "Stubborn-ass woman. No one wanted to face the charging bull."

Eli had to smile. A charging bull for sure. Horns, attitude and all. He wiped a hand over his face, trying hard to overlook the pain enveloping his body. Not an easy feat.

He sighed. "I almost died when I saw her in that bastard's arms."

"You almost died from him stabbing the hell out of you. By the way, you left a nice bruise on Nikki's thigh when you kicked her."

Eli winced. "Damn."

"At least it's over. He's dead and the police have already been to his house. Word is he's been killing for quite a while. Morales said he even has a big box of mementos so hopefully some loved ones will finally get some closure."

"Jesus. How did he get away with it?"

Caelan shrugged and blew out a big breath. He looked almost uncomfortable.

Eli cocked his head. "What's wrong?"

Caelan cleared his throat. "Nothing. I mean, I need to get out of here, get back to Tieran."

"Shit, Cael, get. Go. What the hell are you still standing here for?"

His twin reached up and scratched his head. "I will. Now. I couldn't leave without knowing you were okay."

"I'm fine. Tell me about my nephew then get lost."

Caelan laughed and rubbed his hands together. "He's huge." He spreads his hands apart, way bigger than any baby could be. "Weighed eight pounds, ten ounces."

Eli lifted an eyebrow. "Impressive."

"Tieran wasn't too impressed, but then she'd just pushed it—"

"Stop right there," Eli groaned, showing his brother the palm of his hand. "Don't need to know that much." He paused. "He's doing okay? You give him a name yet?" Caelan and Tieran had only been fighting over it for nine months.

Caelan's grin took over his face. "He's perfect. For a shriveled-up, slimy, red-skinned...thing, I guess. Ten fingers, ten toes, one penis."

"That's a good thing."

"As for the name." Caelan shrugged. "Tieran hasn't decided yet."

"You're leaving it to her? Good God, Cael, my nephew might end up as a Josephus Jehoshaphat if you give her control."

Caelan's bark of laughter made Nikki stir with a moan.

"Get out of here," Eli hissed, "before you wake my mate up."

"Oh, now he doesn't want her to wake up," Caelan said, heading for the door and shaking his head. He stopped in the doorway and braced his hand on the frame. "I think you guys are being released the day after tomorrow, and so will Tieran, so I'll drive everyone home."

Eli turned, trying to get in a more comfortable position. "That's so nice of you, bro, you being the only one able to drive."

"I love you too, E. Get some sleep, smartass."

"Yeah," he mumbled, turning to face Nikki again. He'd come so close to losing her. At that one moment, when her life literally hung in the balance, when she was a few short breaths away from death, he'd felt it. Deep in his soul like someone ripping his insides out.

There was color in her cheeks at least. Dark circles smudged the skin beneath her eyes, blending in with the black lashes lying against them. Her eyes would probably be bloodshot, a result of the strangulation. Eli's breath hitched just thinking about it.

If the fucker wasn't already dead, Eli would make certain he never lived to see another day.

Nikki was too far away. He wanted to go to her, but Caelan was right. He was hurting like a son of a bitch.

What the hell. He eased the metal rail down and gingerly sat, testing the various parts of his body. An IV clung to his hand. He hadn't noticed it before. Following the tube, he saw two bags of fluid hanging from the stand. No time like the present. Eli swung his legs to the side, twisting himself up in the blue material covering his body.

Yanking at it didn't help. The thing was still stuck under his ass. It tightened around his thighs as he slid off the mattress. Damn thing was possessed and trying to prevent him from getting out of bed. He groped at it, freeing it from whatever held it captive, and finally stood on wobbly legs.

He was weaker than he thought. Probably still drugged out of his mind too, even though drugs normally left his system quickly. How much had they given him? Cold air washed down his back. "What the..." He angled his head, and stared at his naked ass. Nice. They'd put him in a fucking dress and hadn't even bothered to tie it shut.

A tingle shot down his spine. Eli half-expected to look up and see Nikki smiling at his predicament. She hadn't moved.

Slowly moving the few feet that separated them, he paused and watched her breathe. Damn she was beautiful. And he loved her. With every fiber of his being.

An urgent need to kiss her took hold and he bent painfully over the railing and laid his lips on her forehead, inhaling her perfect scent. Standing back up proved even more painful and he discovered he had another pressing need.

He glanced up longingly. The bathroom looked about a mile away.

"Fuck. I can make it to the john on my own, damn it." It took him twice as long as he thought it would because his feet and legs didn't seem to want to cooperate and he had to lug the stupid IV pole with him.

Once inside the tiny room, he let the gown fall to the ground. A fucking dress. He shook his head again. Not that he hadn't been in one before, he had. Nine months ago, in fact. Still, it made a man not feel like a man.

A square white bandage covered the left side of his abdomen. A few spots of red seeped through, probably from when he nearly launched himself off the bed earlier. He'd have them look at it in the morning. No use disturbing Nikki for something like this. Another bandage adorned his left pec. Hmm. He didn't remember that.

Eli shrugged, wincing at the pain. *Like you didn't just see the damage done there?* "Moron."

His left arm was also wrapped in white. That one he remembered. Popping the muscles in his neck, he performed the necessary functions, flushed, washed his hands and stared at the blue puddle of fabric on the floor, contemplating it.

Fuck it. If the nurses hadn't already seen all of him, they more than likely would at some point, changing the bandages.

Besides, he knew how much Nikki-Raine liked to be against his skin.

He yanked the pole over the threshold and made his way back to his mate, leaning heavily on the damn pole, much to his disgust. He was weak as a baby.

Speaking of babies, his poor baby still hadn't moved. Fortunately, whenever she'd rolled to her side, she'd left plenty of room for him to get in with her. Unfortunately, she was on the wrong side for him. He'd have to lie on his left side this way, and that wasn't going to happen.

Eli hated having to move her and risk waking her, but damned if he was going to go back to his own bed. He had to hold her, to make sure she was really alive and not some figment of his imagination.

After tugging the blanket off her, he somehow managed to roll Nikki to her other side without her stirring. Feeling heavier and heavier by the minute, Eli eased onto the side of the bed and maneuvered himself behind her. He reached back and yanked the rail back into place and pulled the covers over both of them.

Sweet, sweet heaven. Nikki instinctively wiggled to get closer, burying her ass in his crotch and making his cock come to life.

Aah. This is what he needed. Eli laid his injured arm over her belly then nestled his nose into the crook of her shoulder and inhaled.

Now he could sleep.

Chapter Twenty

Nikki guided Eli with an arm around his waist. The fool was heavier than he looked. She grunted under the strain of holding him up. Didn't help that his naked body was slick with sweat.

"I don't need any more rest." Eli struggled against Nikki's hands as she tried to push him back in his bed.

"Right. That's why you can't walk under your own steam. It's all a delusion. Now, lay your ass down or I swear to God I won't give you sex for a week." She wouldn't last a freaking week. No way. Eli was hers. Forever.

He whimpered and she hid a smile. He must have believed her because he collapsed onto the mattress and let her pull the covers over his body.

"I feel like a damned baby."

She chuckled at his grouchiness. He could be a baby all he wanted as long as he was still here with her. Nikki shuddered, thinking about what could have happened in that closet.

"You sound like one too. Why tempt reopening the wound when you can lie here like a good boy and let it heal? And if you ever take on a psycho killer again, I'll kill you myself." Damn, she'd never forget waking up to see them lifting him onto a stretcher. There'd been so much blood. She'd been so afraid he wouldn't live through the blood loss alone.

He growled. She lifted an eyebrow.

"You don't scare me, Eli."

He dropped his head to the pillow and groaned. His cock tented the thin sheet. How on Earth could he be hard at a time like this? Weak as an infant, and still horny. She shook her head, but couldn't resist licking her lips. "Do I look like Superman to you?" he grumbled.

Nikki looked at his face. His nostrils were flared and his eyes were wide. She swallowed and felt her cheeks burn at being caught checking him out.

She lifted her chin. "I don't know what you mean," she huffed, busying herself with getting his shoes off.

"You couldn't make it a week, sweetheart," he taunted.

"Watch me." She'd have to find some kind of resolve somewhere if she wanted to make it through the night.

Now it was Eli's turn to swallow. "I don't wanna sleep anymore."

"Quit whining. Besides, if you're really good, maybe I'll reward you."

From the corner of her eye she saw his cock jump beneath the sheet. She wiggled her eyebrows at him before turning her attention to his groin and licking her lips again.

"Christ, don't do that, Nikki-Raine. Just thinking about what that sweet little tongue can do makes me harder than hell." He rubbed a hand over his bare chest. The T-shirt he'd worn home had left him itchy and feeling confined. Not to mention it was rubbing on his wounds and making him surly. They'd barely hit the front door and he'd stripped it off. That and his pants. Good thing they'd been alone or somebody might have gotten quite a peep show.

Nikki reached for the tent in the sheet. Eli dug his hands beneath his pillow and waited, breath held in anticipation of her touch. "Damn little tease," he breathed. "I'll get you for this."

She smiled. "You and what army?"

"I won't need a fucking army, sweetheart. Just my cock buried deep inside your tiny wet pussy'll be enough."

Nikki's breath caught a split second before her fingers wrapped around his circumference. He hissed through his teeth and threw his head back in what she hoped was sheer bliss.

His abs jumped as she slowly inched the sheet she'd just pulled over him back off. Nikki released him long enough to uncover the steel rod she'd been holding and the cotton slid along his length with wicked intent. He gritted his teeth and his triceps bunched like he was trying to keep from grabbing her and throwing her to the bed so he could fuck her like she needed to be fucked. At least that's what she wanted to think.

Her fingers returned, cold on his heated cock.

"So soft," she whispered as she started pumping him. "So hard."

His teeth lengthened and he hissed. Her thumb brushed over the tip, smearing the small drop of pre-come that seeped out.

"Fuuuck." Eli lifted his head to stare at her.

She lowered her head in an agonizingly slow manner, trying to tease him. From the way he licked his lips and propped himself on his elbows to watch her descent, she would say it was working. Nikki's hair fell over his hips. She hoped it blocked his view and increased the anticipation. His hands fisted the sheets and his body was a rigid line beneath her. Thank God the painkillers had left his injuries numb. He'd probably be hurting later though. It was a wonder he could even feel his cock, let alone get it up, but oh damn.

218

She breathed over the swollen head and he groaned. "Holy mother..."

Her lips quivered against it as she chuckled. When the tip of her tongue traced the slit he nearly shot off the bed. Nikki sat back, throwing her hair over her shoulder and trying unsuccessfully not to laugh.

"Anxious?"

"Stop teasing a wounded man, sweetheart."

She rolled her eyes, but smiled, and then bent over him again.

Sweeping her hot tongue across him made him lift his hips. Nikki enveloped him in her mouth, and sucked strongly. She moved, bobbing her head up and down, drawing on him. His balls tightened, readying themselves to explode.

It didn't take long. Sweat beaded on his forehead, his lip bled where a sharp canine bit through it and she could tell his heart pounded. Her hair tickled his abdomen and thighs with every sweep.

"Baby..." He pursed his lips. She met his eyes with her defiance-filled ones. "Stop. Stop, or I'm going...I'm gonna..."

She added her hand to the base of his cock and his eyes rolled back.

"Nikki-Raine." With a guttural cry he came. Hot spurts of semen shot into the back of her throat and still she squeezed and sucked, milking him for all he was worth. His belly contracted and seized with each discharge.

Eli collapsed, his chest heaving. Her tongue laved his insatiable cock from root to tip, bathing it with a mixture of come and saliva, lapping up everything. His chest heaved with each effort to draw a breath.

Nikki released his cock with an audible pop and pulled the sheet over his body. His fingers slackened their death grip and he sank into the mattress. She rained small kisses on his skin just above the sheet and tucked it around his chest. Her lips moved up his throat, around his jaw, over his face, soothing the tenseness away.

"I love you, my mate." His drugged announcement barely reached her ears.

Nikki reared back to look at him. He'd already fallen asleep. She thought about all the time she had now to devote herself to showing him how much she loved him. She took a deep breath, enjoying the freedom that came with it. Now she could finally put this last year behind her. She'd never forget her friends or what had happened to them and she still had a trial to get through for the three men who'd attacked her, but she'd do it. With Eli by her side, she'd be fine. Nikki had no doubt he would see to her happiness just as she would do for him.

She flipped the hair off his forehead. "I love you too. Always."

About the Author

Annmarie McKenna lives with her husband and four kids in the Midwest. Throw in a dog and a cat and she's well over her limit for the average family. Luckily, writing fantasies has proven to be an excellent way to de-stress from her daily life of being a cleaning woman, chauffeur, cook and mom. Okay, cleaning woman—not so much. She leaves that to her hubby. Now if only she could figure out how to de-stress her kids, she'd be all set. To learn more about Annmarie, please visit www.annmariemckenna.com or her tries-to-keep-up-with-it-but-rarely-succeeds blog, www.annmariemckenna.blogspot.com. She'd love to hear from you. Send her an email to annmarmck@yahoo.com.

Look for these titles

Even with her shaky past, Aislinn can't help but to secretly want Kyle. When she witnesses his death in a vision, how can she tell him without giving away her secret or her lust?

Two Sighted
© 2007 Annmarie McKenna

Aislinn Campbell is a clairvoyant, the latest in a long line of first-born daughters to the previous first-born daughter. All of them have fiery red hair and a second sight. Hiding from her ex in the presence of a sexy ex-military millionaire seems the safest way to start over. Until she "sees" his death.

Kyle Turner III has been keeping a close eye on Aislinn. There's nothing he doesn't know about his personal assistant, including her secret and ugly past. He also wants her in his bed more than his next breath. When he receives an anonymous warning that something might happen at his annual Fourth of July bash, he doesn't take it lightly. He knows exactly who sent the warning and he knows she's being watched by her bastard of an ex.

After he's injured in an accident, Kyle isn't about to leave Aislinn unprotected for a second. He coaxes her into more than just tending to his wounds. Because making Aislinn believe in him and her together far outweighs anything her ex can dish out.

Available now in ebook from Samhain Publishing.

GREAT cheap fun

Discover eBooks!
THE FASTEST WAY TO GET THE HOTTEST NAMES

Get your favorite authors on your favorite reader, long before they're
out in print! Ebooks from Samhain go wherever you go, and work with
whatever you carry—Palm, PDF, Mobi, and more.

Samhain
Publishing, Ltd

WWW.SAMHAINPUBLISHING.COM

LaVergne, TN USA
04 February 2010
172117LV00003B/71/A